Tainted Love

The Love Series
Part Two

Emma Keene

ISBN: 1495406105
ISBN-13: 978-1495406102

This is a work of fiction. Similarities to real people, places,
or events are entirely coincidental.

DEDICATION

This book is dedicated to my husband and our two dogs. They keep me sane while I write. Their distractions are always welcome. I love you three, you're the best family I could have ever asked for.

CONTENTS

ACKNOWLEDGMENTS

I would like to acknowledge all the hard work and hours put in by Outfox Digital Publishing. Thank you so much, you did a wonderful job and I can't wait to see what we can do together in the future.

CHAPTER ONE

I look over at my mom and give her a dirty look. She's too busy doing something on her phone to even notice. When did she get a Smartphone? I shouldn't be surprised, pretty much everything about her has changed since I last saw her.

I look out my window as we leave Greenville, heading toward Salem. She mentioned that a plane was waiting, but the closest airport is three hours away. This is going to be a long ride.

"I didn't want this, trust me," she says.

I ignore her. If she didn't want this, then why the heck is she making me leave? It still feels unreal. I can't believe when I woke up this morning the first thing I saw was Logan and now... now I don't know when I'll see him again. I force myself not to cry. I'm not about to give her the satisfaction.

"I know you probably don't believe me, but it's the truth."

She's right, I don't believe her. I'll never believe anything she ever tells me. Not after what she put our family through and especially not after today.

We sit in silence for the next few minutes. I'm not

saying a word to her and I think she's finally starting to understand that.

"How much longer, Tony?"

"About twenty minutes," he says, glancing over his shoulder at us.

She lets out a sigh. Now I'm just confused. I assumed that we were going to an airport. Where could we be going that's only twenty minutes away?

Out of the corner of my eye I can see that my mom is still on her phone. There was a time that I would ask her who she was texting, but now… I don't care and she probably wouldn't tell me anyway.

I pull out my phone so I can text Logan. There's already a message from him.

I miss you.

I want to cry. Leaving Logan is going to be the worst part about all of this.

I miss you.

I stare out the window as I wait for his reply. I feel my phone vibrate in my hand and I look at the screen.

I can't lose you.

You won't. I'm going to get away from here as soon as possible.

It crosses my mind that I could always just refuse to go with her or try to run once the car stops, but what good would that really do? I probably wouldn't make it very far and I have a feeling she would just call the cops on me.

Don't do anything you'll regret.

He must have known what I was thinking. I know he's right. I need to convince her to let me leave or I'm going to be stuck in Los Angeles until my birthday. There's no way I can last that long with my mom and without Logan.

Am I really going to have to live with her until my birthday?

As if right on cue, my mom lets out a little giggle. I shoot her an irritated glance, but she doesn't even look up from her phone.

Who is she? It's still hard for me to look at her and see my mother. It's like she's a completely different person in such a short amount of time. Is this what happens when you move to Hollywood?

I don't know that you have any other choice.

My heart sinks. I know he's right, it's just so hard to swallow. I feel like Logan is the only thing in my life that has gone right in the last couple of months and she is taking me away from him.

I already need to kiss you.

I hate my mom.

I turn my head just enough so that I can glare at her while I wait for his reply. She smiles as she looks at her phone. I never thought I would feel this much anger for another human being, especially for her.

Me too.

The car turns down a dirt road I've never noticed before, but probably have passed a thousand times. We are less than thirty minutes outside of Greenville and I didn't think there was really much of anything out here. Where the heck are we going?

We pass a row of tall trees and cross into a massive open field. The dirt road turns into pavement as we drive. I peek around the front headrest and see a plane. This is definitely not what I was expecting. I had no idea there was even an airport here.

Tony brings the car to a stop just shy of the plane, hops out of the car and opens my mom's door. I open my own door and get out. He opens the trunk and grabs my bags before I can protest.

The plane has a pointed nose, a blue stripe down the side, on the tail it says 'G650' and the tips of the wings are upturned. It looks fancy, with an engine on either side near the tail, but it's not like any plane I've ever seen. It's pretty small and just has eight windows down the side.

My mom walks up the stairs and into the plane. As my hand touches the railing I freeze. I've never been on a plane before. We could never afford it and had to always drive when we took one of our rare family vacations. Now that I'm thinking about it, is this actually safe? This plane seems so small. My mom pokes her head back out of the door and glares at me.

"Amy, get on this plane right now."

I take a deep breath, close my eyes, and lift my right foot onto the first step. I force myself to climb the rest of the way and finally open my eyes as I step through the door.

It's much nicer inside than a regular plane, or what I think a regular plane is like on the inside. The only knowledge I have of planes is from movies and TV.

I pass through an area that looks like a kitchen on the left and there's a bathroom on the right. Instead of rows and rows of seats, there are just six large chairs that look almost like recliners. The floors are carpeted, there are wood accents along the walls and built in cup holders.

My mom is sitting in the first chair on my right. I walk by her without making eye contact and sit in the last chair on the left, trying to put myself as far away from her as possible.

A woman comes out of the cockpit and closes the door behind herself. She is wearing a gray skirt suit, a white shirt and has her brown hair in a bun. She opens a cabinet in the small kitchen up front and takes out a bottle of champagne. The flight attendant grabs a glass from another cabinet and walks over to my mom and pours her a drink.

I look out the window and watch the grass that lines the landing strip as the wind gently blows.

"Miss?"

I turn my attention to the flight attendant. She hands me a bottle of water and I put it in my cup holder.

"Would you like me to bring you a snack before we take off?"

I shake my head. The last thing I'm thinking about right now is eating.

"My name is Tina, by the way, and if you need anything

during the flight just let me know."

"Thanks."

She smiles at me and walks away. I pick up the bottle of water and look out the window as I twist the cap off. It's still weird that I'm on a plane, in the middle of nowhere. Not to mention, I never imagined that the first time I flew on a plane it was going to be a private jet.

I feel like if this was any other day, and I was with any other person, I would be so excited.

I hear a whine, coming from outside, that is getting louder and louder as the engines start. It turns into a roar and the plane starts to creep forward. The plane turns so that it is straight on the runway and it starts to pick up speed.

The nose of the plane lifts off the ground and the tail follows. The sheer force pins me to my seat. I look out the window briefly but the ground is so blurred that it makes me feel nauseous.

The plane turns to the right as we continue to climb. I look to the front of the plane and see the flight attendant sitting in a seat that folds out of the wall near the kitchen. She smiles at me as if she can tell that this is my first time on a plane. I force myself to smile back.

After a few minutes the plane levels out and I feel like I can breathe again. I have no idea why anyone would want to travel like this if they had any other choice.

When the plane levels out again I look out the window just in time to see Salem passing below us. It seems so small from up here. Just looking at it reminds me of Logan, and the time I thought we were going to spend there together. I have to look away.

Tina is up and moving around, doing something in the kitchen. I pull out my phone to text Logan. There's a message from him waiting for me.

We will get through this, I promise.

"You won't get service up here," Tina says.

I look down at my phone. She's right, I have no service

at all. I set it on the chair between my legs.

"Here," she says, holding out a steaming towel. "Wipe your hands with this, it's warm and it feels really good."

She smiles at me as I take the towel. She was right, it feels amazing. Tina waits for me to finish with the towel and then takes it back. She smiles again and then heads back to the front of the plane.

I pick up my phone and look at it again, expecting that I will magically have service, but I don't. I shut it off to save the battery and put it in my pocket. I let out a sigh and look out the window. It's amazing to watch the ground as we fly above it. It all looks so small and insignificant, which is how I'm feeling right about now.

I have no idea how long this flight is going to take, but I already know that it's going to feel like a lifetime. I close my eyes and try to push every thought out of my mind.

CHAPTER TWO

A light touch on my shoulder wakes me up. It takes me a minute to realize that I'm sleeping on a plane and it's Tina waking me up. I can't believe I actually fell asleep.

"I just wanted to let you know that we will be landing in a few minutes and I didn't want it to startle you awake."

"Thanks."

She smiles at me and heads back to the front of the plane. Tina takes her seat and flashes me another smile before my mom demands her attention.

I look out the window. I can see cars again, driving on packed roads, but they still look tiny. All of a sudden the ground disappears and we are flying over water. I gasp and hold my breath.

"It's fine, we have to go over the water so that we can make our approach from the west," Tina says.

I nod and let the air out of my lungs. The plane banks sharply and we head back in the direction we just came from. I hear a loud clunk from the plane and I look at Tina. Her smile tells me that everything is fine. I don't believe that a sound like that could be OK. Is something wrong with the plane? My mind fills with thoughts of planes crashing to Earth and bursting into flames.

I close my eyes and start to pray.

The plane shakes and I feel like I'm being pushed forward in my seat. I open my eyes, just a little, and look outside. My heart is still racing. We are on the ground and it looks like we are slowing down.

I look out the window and see other small planes parked just off the runway, but I don't see any larger planes. I wonder where we are. The plane almost comes to a stop and turns into an empty hanger. The engines power down and Tina gets out of her seat and goes to open the door.

I check to see that I have my phone and my purse and head toward the front of the plane. My mom gets up, and without even looking in my direction gets off the plane. As I reach the front, Tina steps aside and smiles at me.

"Thanks, have a good day," she says.

"Thank you."

I climb down the stairs and take a deep breath of fresh air. I never thought I would be so happy to just have my feet on the ground.

A black car, similar to the one that drove us to the airport, pulls into the hanger and stops. A man gets out and nods at my mom before grabbing my two duffel bags out of the plane and putting them in the trunk of the car.

"It's so good to see you, Ricardo, the driver I had in Greenville was just... he was horrific."

"It's good to see you, too, Ms. K."

Hearing my mom called Ms. sounds so strange. I never thought I would hear it.

My mom stands at the passenger side back door of the car waiting for Ricardo to finish loading the bags. What, is she too good to open a door now? He closes the trunk and hurries over to open her door. The look on his face says that he doesn't want to disappoint her. Is this who she's turned in to?

She gets in the car and I follow. By the time I buckle my seatbelt, she has her phone out and is holding it up to her ear.

"Hey… yeah, we just landed."

I take out my phone. I need to text Logan back, I'm sure he wondered what happened. There's a text waiting on my phone from him.

Is everything OK?

"Sure, I'm meeting Nicole at seven, so I might be kind of late."

I wonder who she's on the phone with. Is it the guy she left Dad for?

Ricardo climbs into the driver's seat and starts the car. We pull out of the airplane hangar and head down a side road. I turn my attention back to my phone.

Sorry, we got on a plane just outside of Greenville and we just landed.

"Alright… love you, too."

She hangs up her phone and turns to me. I turn my head and look out the window. I have no desire to make eye contact with her. I guess she must have been talking to whoever she left Dad for. I have no desire to meet him.

We take a right onto a main road. We come to a stop and I look at the street signs. We are on Santa Monica Boulevard, which sounds strangely familiar. The light turns green and we go straight, passing under a bridge for a freeway.

My phone vibrates and I look down and see a text from Logan.

I didn't know there was even an airport near Greenville.

I didn't either, it was more like just a runway.

I look out the window as we stop at another light. I thought the traffic in Salem was bad, especially after moving from Greenville, but this is just insane. There are cars everywhere. I see a sign, on the opposite corner, that's dark blue with yellow letters that says 'Beverly Hills.'

Where are you now?

I blink and look at the sign again as Ricardo drives through the intersection.

I'm in Beverly Hills.

Under normal circumstances I would be excited, and a little star struck, to be in Beverly Hills. It's weird to be in a place that you've seen on TV and hear about your whole life. I look out the window half expecting to see a movie star walking down the street. My phone vibrates.

Crazy. What's it like?

It looks like anywhere, there's just a lot more people.

As I'm texting, Ricardo turns left. There aren't any more businesses lining the street. There are houses instead, some of which are the same size as the ones in Salem but the rest are massive. I've never seen anything like them in real life. I look down at my phone.

Really? I thought it would be different. I'm not sure how, but I thought movie stars didn't live like the rest of us.

I may have spoken too soon. Ricardo turns the car into a driveway and waits for the automatic gate to swing open. He pulls through and into a circle driveway and stops in front of one of the biggest houses I've ever seen in my life.

It's a two story concrete house, with a lot of windows facing the street. It looks very boxy and modern, but I think it looks cool.

Is this where she lives? Did she leave my dad because she met some rich, Hollywood guy in Greenville? That's the only explanation.

Ricardo gets out of the car and opens the door for my mom. I open my own door and step out. She spins around and shoots me a dirty look. Whatever, I can let myself out of a car.

I go to the trunk to get my bags, but Ricardo looks at me. He has a pleading look on his face, as if he's asking me not to get the bags and I step aside. Ricardo nods toward the door, where my mom is standing waiting for me.

When I reach the front door she lowers her sunglasses and glares at me.

"We pay him a lot of money, let him do his job."

She turns and walks inside. I seriously doubt *she's*

paying him anything. It's weird… it seems like she settled into this new life of hers really quickly. I glance over my shoulder as I walk in the door and see that Ricardo is right behind me.

My mom is to the left, standing next to a staircase, when I walk in the door. In front of me there is what looks like a living room, with large windows that look out to the backyard, and to the right is a formal looking dining room.

"Ricardo, put her in the back corner bedroom. The empty one."

He nods, walks by her and up the stairs. She turns to me and just stares.

"Well… you better follow him if you want to know where your room is."

I just look at her, wondering what happened to my mom… to the woman who raised me. I wonder if there's any of her left inside of the Hollywood bitch that's standing in front of me. I grit my teeth and follow Ricardo up the stairs. He waits for me when he reaches the top and then walks straight down a long hallway.

There are doors on both sides of the hall but all of them are closed. Modern art covers the walls. It mostly looks like something a kid could have done and I'm sure it was probably expensive.

Ricardo stops in front of a door on the left side of the hall, near the end, and sets down my bags. I look to my left and see a staircase. Wow, two staircases in one house? That seems a little excessive.

I follow Ricardo into the room and my jaw drops. If this is what my room looks like I can't even imagine how nice the master must be. The room is almost twice the size of my room in Greenville with a king size bed against the wall, with windows on either side of it. I've never slept in a king size before. There's a built-in closet along the open wall and a door which I assume leads to a bathroom.

Ricardo sets my bags down on the bed, pulls the curtains open and turns to me.

"Is there anything else, Miss Amy?"

"No, I'm fine, thanks."

He nods and leaves the room.

I walk over to the door and open it and walk into my very own bathroom, something I've never had before. A smile crosses my face for the first time since leaving Logan. There is a large shower, a beautiful vanity and sink and a toilet in the corner. Everything is beautiful and looks really expensive.

I sit down on the bed and pull out my phone. I guess I got caught up in the house because I forgot to text Logan back.

Hey, sorry, just got to the house and got settled into my new room.

I hit send and look around the room while I wait for a reply. The paintings on the wall match the rest of the house. I wonder how much all of this art cost. It seems a little nuts to put this kind of stuff in a room that is obviously not used most of the time.

My phone vibrates.

It's all good, I figured it was something like that. How's the house? Is it a mansion?

Now that he mentions it, I guess that this house would probably qualify as a mansion. I haven't seen the whole thing yet but based on the outside, and what I have seen inside, I would say that this counts as a mansion.

It's giant and really nice. My room is huge. I have a king size bed!

I bounce up and down on the bed to test it out. It's really comfortable, too. I'm actually kind of looking forward to going to sleep tonight.

Good, I hope that it makes your stay there a little more bearable.

I still want to get out of here as soon as possible.

There is a knock on my bedroom door. I roll my eyes. I wonder what the heck my mom wants now. I debate just ignoring it but there is a second knock. I get up, walk to the door and open it.

Standing in the hall is a woman, dressed like a maid. She smiles at me but doesn't say anything.

"Yes?" I say.

"Sorry to bother you, Miss Amy. What would you like to have for dinner?"

"What?"

"Dinner, what would you like me to make you?"

My phone vibrates in my hand, but I don't look down at it.

"Uh... I have no idea."

She looks down at her feet as if she did something wrong.

"I'm sorry, I'm... I'm just not used to any of *this*."

She looks up at me with a confused look on her face.

"I come from a small town. I've never *seen* a house this big, let alone lived in one. I'm just a little overwhelmed right now. So make whatever you feel like, I'm sure that it will be good."

She nods and smiles at me before walking away and heading down the staircase that's just to the right of my door.

Crazy. A driver and a cook? This guy must be making some serious money. I wonder if he was one of the stars of the movie? Or maybe a producer?

I close my bedroom door, sit back down on the bed and read the text from Logan.

I know, but unless you can convince your mom to let you leave, you might as well make the best of it and enjoy living in a mansion.

He's right. I do want to get out of here as soon as possible, but I guess I should be thankful that at least I get to spend my short time in L.A. in a nice house. If I think about it, it's a lot better than being one of those kids who has to live in a crappy apartment after their parents get divorced. Still, I wouldn't be in this position at all if it wasn't for her.

Yeah, I still need to get out of here. I miss you terribly. I can't do a month of this.

I set my phone down on the bed, get up and walk over to the window. The back yard is massive, much larger than anything I've ever seen. There's a massive pool in the middle of it that looks like it could double as a pool for the Olympics. A hot tub, that's as big as most pools I've seen, sits next to the pool. Perfectly manicured hedges run around the entire property line and large trees dot the yard.

I hear my phone vibrate and I sit back down on the bed to pick it up.

I miss you, too. Just try to remember this is temporary. We'll be together soon.

I know, you're right. We are supposed to be together, I just know it.

I have to go to a football meeting, will you be around later?

My heart sinks a little. I never want to stop talking to him, especially now that we are so far away from each other.

Yeah, I'll be here. I don't plan on going anywhere.

Talk to you later.

It pains me to not be able to text him. Hopefully his meeting won't last very long. I guess this will give me a chance to text Jess. I miss her, too, just not as much as Logan. Not to mention I haven't even told her yet that I left. Everything happened so fast that I didn't get a chance.

Jess, sorry I didn't text you earlier, but I had to leave. My mom showed up in Greenville and she made me leave.

Hopefully she's not at work yet. It's getting kind of late plus there's the time difference. Thankfully she replies almost instantly, which brings a little bit of a smile to my face.

What??? That's crazy! Where are you now?

I almost laugh as I read the text in her voice.

I'm in L.A., staying at her boyfriend's house.

Is he nice?

I have no idea, I haven't met him yet.

It is kind of weird that I really have no idea who he is and I know nothing about him, yet here I am sitting in his house. Well, I mean, I guess I know that he works in the movie industry and that he was in Greenville for that movie they filmed, but that doesn't tell me much about him.

Crazy. Well, hopefully he isn't an ass.

The thought hadn't crossed my mind. I guess that it's a good question though. My mom certainly has changed a lot in such a short amount of time so it's quite possible that he could be an ass, too.

I really hope that's not the case.

Yeah... I hope he's alright.

Ugh. I'm kind of not looking forward to meeting him. Not that I really was before, but now... now I don't know what to expect and I have a sick feeling that he might be hard to be around. My phone vibrates.

For sure. Listen, I want to catch up some more and I want to hear more about how this all happened, but I've really got to get to work. Can I text you later?

Yeah, for sure. Have a good shift.

I set my phone on the bedside table and walk over to the window. I wish I could have talked to Jess some more, I need to figure all of this out and I can't keep dumping it all on Logan. I feel like he doesn't deserve that.

I stare out the window and let my thoughts drift, trying to not think about my current predicament.

CHAPTER THREE

A knock on my bedroom door brings me back to reality. I blink and realize that I have no idea how long I've been standing at the window, but it's dark now.

There's a second knock. I'm surprised my mom didn't just walk right in. I walk over to the door, take a deep breath and prepare myself to face her, and open the door.

I'm surprised, again, when instead of my mom it's the cook who's standing at my door.

"Sorry to disturb you, Miss Amy, but dinner is ready."

"Oh... of course, no it's fine...."

"If you are ready to eat, you can just follow me."

I smile at her and she turns and walks toward the stairs. I close my door and hurry to catch up to her. The staircase is identical to the one on the other side of the house, but instead of leading into an open area, it leads to a hallway with three doors. I follow her through the middle one, which leads us into the far end of the kitchen.

Where I'm standing, there's a dining table with six chairs, two on each of the long sides and one on each end, and at the far end of the massive room is the appliances and the main part of the kitchen. The ends of the table are set, but I don't see my mom anywhere.

"You can sit here," she says, pointing at one of the chairs at the end.

I sit down as she walks over to the kitchen island. She gets a plate and brings it back and sets it down in front of me.

"What would you like to drink?"

"Water is fine, thanks."

She nods and walks away. It's weird to have someone wait on me for a change.

I look down at the plate. There is a large steak, which looks like it's cooked on the very rare side, some mashed potatoes and steamed broccoli. She comes back with my water and basket of bread and sets them on the table.

"What's your name?"

"Gina."

"Nice to meet you, Gina."

She smiles at me and turns to walk away.

"Gina?"

"Yes?" she says, turning around to face me.

"Is my mom eating with me?"

I look to the other end of the table. I'm not looking forward to sitting across from her. I guess I'm going to have to talk to her eventually, I just don't know if I'm ready yet.

"Oh, no… she went out a little while ago, but Mr. Baldwin will be joining you for dinner. He just came home and went upstairs to get changed."

She turns and walks over to the stove.

Mr. Baldwin? As in Dexter Baldwin? The director? Wow, I guess my mom met him when they were filming the movie in Greenville. It's hard to imagine her dating a famous, successful Hollywood director. It's just… so not her. She's mom… she's a teacher… she's not the girlfriend of a famous movie director.

I guess I'm going to be meeting him. I try to swallow but my throat is dry. I reach for my glass and take a long drink of water.

Gina walks back to the table and sets down a plate on the other end that looks identical to mine. I watch as she opens one of the cabinets, which is actually a fridge full of only drinks, and opens a beer and sets it down on the table.

In addition to the door I came through, there are four other doors in the kitchen and this eating area. I find myself looking at each, over and over, wondering which one he's going to come through. My heart starts to beat faster.

While I'm looking at the door right in front of me it opens and in he walks. He flashes a smile at me and then looks at Gina while pulling out his chair.

"Hey, Gina, how are you?"

"I'm good, Mr. Baldwin, how are you?"

I watch as he picks up his napkin, shakes it out and puts it on his lap. His movements look so fluid. He picks up his beer and takes a sip before answering Tina.

"I had a crazy day… we're in the middle of editing and the studio is trying to force me to finish this thing for a Christmas release… and I just don't know if it's going to happen."

She just smiles at him and shakes her head. He shrugs.

"You'll figure out a way to make them happy, Mr. Baldwin, you always do."

He takes another sip of his beer and then turns to me. I feel like my heart skips a beat… like I'm under inspection.

"So… Amy, how was the flight?"

"It was OK I guess."

"Just OK? Hmm… well… usually people are a little impressed by the private jet."

I try to swallow but I can't.

"Sorry," he says. "That sounded bad… don't look so unnerved. My hope was that you would find this… transition a little easier if you got to travel like a movie star."

He smiles and winks at me. When he looks into my

eyes, I feel the same calm as when Logan touches me. I smile at him. He seems alright so far.

"Yeah... It seemed really nice. I just don't have anything to compare it to."

A confused look crosses his face as he picks up his fork and knife.

"What do you mean?"

I pick up mine and watch him start cutting his steak. I skewer a broccoli crown on my fork before I answer him.

"I've never been on a plane before, so all I know is what I've seen on TV and in movies."

His eyes grow wide as he chews a bite of steak. I eat my broccoli and go for a bite of potatoes next.

"Wow, really?"

I nod my head. I feel a little embarrassed admitting it, especially to someone with access to a private jet.

"Well... you are completely ruined from now on. There's no sense in ever flying commercial after you've flown private."

I have a feeling he's right. I also know that I probably will never get to fly on a private jet again. I can't even imagine how much that would cost.

I look down and realize I've eaten all of the potatoes. They were amazing. I reach for a piece of bread, and then offer the basket to Mr. Baldwin.

"No, thanks. I'm doing the no gluten thing. It's brutal."

I smile. I can't believe I was worried if he was going to be an ass... he's really nice... he seems like such a normal person. I set the bread down and take a bite of the chewy goodness. Everything so far tastes amazing.

"So, is your room alright? Do you need anything else?"

"No... I think I'm OK."

He smiles and I smile back. I finally cut a piece of the steak and put it in my mouth. I close my eyes as I chew and try to forget how rare it looks. It practically melts. It's amazing.

"Well, if you think of anything just ask one of the staff

or me."

"Thanks, Mr. Baldwin."

"You don't have to call me Mr. Baldwin. Mr. Baldwin was my father. You can call me Dex."

I smile at him and he smiles back, while still chewing a piece of steak. He's really sweet.

"Alright, Dex."

I take another bite of the steak, keeping my eyes open this time. I reach for my water, which I notice is empty, but before I can even stand up Gina is next to me with a water pitcher.

"Thank you."

"Also, Amy, please feel free to use the pool, hot tub, game room and theater… whatever. None of it really gets used very often, so enjoy."

"Thanks."

"Did you get a tour yet?"

I shake my head. Dex frowns and sets his napkin on the table, next to his plate, and stands up.

"C'mon, that just won't do."

He nods his head toward the door he came through and I stand up. I follow him through the door and into the living room that I saw when I first got here.

"So, this is the living room, which I pretty much never go into."

He walks through the room and into the entryway. He points to the dining room.

"Dining room, which I never use. So no point in going in there."

He smiles and I follow him toward the stairs. There's a door to the right of the stairs, but he walks by it.

"What's in there?"

"That's the one room I use, so I want to save that for last."

I wonder what it could be. We go up the stairs and turn to the left. Dex opens a double door and we walk into another hall. There is a door on the right and another one straight ahead.

"This is the master."

He opens the door at the end of the hall and we walk into his room.

I never knew that a bedroom could be so large. The main part of the room is easily twice as large as my room and there's two openings on the far end that lead into another part of the room. There is a huge bed, it looks larger than a king, against one wall and the other wall is all windows that face the backyard.

"This is the bathroom."

We go in and my jaw almost drops. There are two sinks in front of a massive mirror that takes up an entire wall, a huge shower that looks like seven or eight people could fit in it and a tub that looks more like a hot tub.

"Nice," I say.

"Yeah… it's not too bad. One of these days I'll probably rip it out and redo it."

I can't imagine tearing out something so beautiful and expensive. I follow Dex out of the bathroom.

"That's the library over there."

He points to the two openings on either side of the far wall. We leave the bedroom and go back down the hall toward my room.

"These two doors on the right are guest rooms and this on the left is the game room."

He opens the door to the game room and we go in. It's fairly large, not as big as the master but bigger than my bedroom. There is a TV against one wall, some couches, a pool table and some stand-up arcade games against the back wall.

"So, feel free to use any of this whenever you want."

"Thanks."

I don't know that I will, but it's nice of him to offer. I might watch some TV though.

"That's kind of it for up here."

We go down the staircase that leads to the kitchen. Dex

points to the door right in front of us when we reach the bottom.

"This is the garage. Do you have your license?"

I shake my head.

"Really? How come?"

"I guess I never saw a reason to get it… my parents needed both of the cars for work and I could walk to school."

I didn't want to admit that it was a money issue. I would have loved to have my own car, especially for when I went away to college, but it was never financially feasible for my family.

"Well… if you want to get your license now you can use one of my cars. If not, Ricardo can give you a ride wherever you need to go. Just ask Gina for his phone number and give him a call if you need to go somewhere. Do you have a phone?"

"Yeah, I do."

"Good, so that should work then. I know it's not as fun having someone drive you around, I remember those days, so if you do want to get your license just let me know and I'll get a driving instructor."

Wow, that's really generous of him. He's right, it would be nice to have the freedom that comes with having a driver's license and a car.

"Thank you, I might take you up on that."

He smiles at me. Dex walks toward a double glass door that leads out back, opens it and waits for me to go through. He closes the door behind us and leads toward the pool.

"So, this is the pool and the hot tub area. You can use them whenever you want. There's a supply closet at the bottom of the stairs, near the door we just came through, and there's towels in there."

The hot tub looks really tempting but I don't own a swimsuit. I guess maybe I can find a store near here and buy one.

"Let's go back inside and I'll show you the one room I do actually use."

We go back through the same door and walk through the kitchen. Gina is just finishing cleaning up and flashes me a smile. Everyone is so nice, so far. Now that I think about it, the only one who's been weird is my mom.

Dex pauses in front of the door, smiles at me and pushes it open. I walk into the room after him and darkness envelops me. Before my eyes can start to adjust, Dex flicks the switch on the wall and the theater lights come on.

"Sorry if that hurt your eyes."

"No, I'm fine."

"Good, it just doesn't have the same wow factor if you can see that it's a theater."

I nod my head and look around the room. It's pretty impressive. The screen takes up the entire wall at the far end of the room. The floor is sloped to provide the thirty or so seats a good view.

"It's… really nice."

"Thanks, I like to come in here late at night and watch movies. You're also welcome to use this room if you want."

"Thanks."

I look around the room again and notice a shelf on one of the walls with awards on it. I walk over to it.

"Is that?"

"Yeah, I won it for best director five years ago."

Wow. I knew that he was successful… I just didn't realize he was *that* successful. I guess that's why everyone made such a big deal when he was in Greenville.

I turn around and face him. He smiles at me. He's the exact opposite of what I thought he was going to be like. I always had this perception of Hollywood types, which my mom confirmed, but Dex is nothing like that. He's just so… normal.

He turns and heads over to a giant stand of electronics

that sit along the back wall.

"Take a seat, I want to show you what it's like."

I sit down somewhere in the middle of the theater and wait. The screen in front of me powers up and Dex dims the lights. It feels almost like sitting in an actual movie theater. I can't believe anyone would actually have this in their house.

Dex sits down next to me as the movie starts. There aren't any credits or anything, it just starts. I wonder what he put on.

It doesn't take long for the movie to take all the air out of my lungs. The first scene takes place in Greenville. Every emotion I've felt in the last couple of days comes rushing back and I start to cry.

"Are you alright?"

I stand up and run out of the room. I take the stairs right outside the theater door and don't stop running until my bedroom door is closed and locked. I sit down with my back against the door and put my head in my hands.

I feel like I've been hypnotized by him. It was like the whole time we were having dinner he had me so distracted that I forgot that he broke up my family. I can't believe it. Then he shows me his beautiful house and then plays a movie of Greenville for me.

I was wrong about Dex. He's no different from my mom. He doesn't care at all that he broke up my family.

"Amy?"

He knocks on my door.

"Can you open the door so we can talk?"

I stand up and walk over to my bed. I have nothing to say to him. I take my earbuds out of my purse and plug them into my phone. I put them in and crank up my music.

I hear one last knock on the door as I close my eyes and lose myself in the music.

CHAPTER FOUR

My phone vibrates as I get a text. I look down at it, hoping that it's Logan. It's from Jess and even though I was looking forward to talking to her I'm a little disappointed.

Hey, I just got home from work. How are you?

I didn't realize it was so late. I guess I was listening to music for a few hours.

Eh, not that great. I had dinner with my mom's new boyfriend.

I still can't believe Dex. He totally pulled the wool over my eyes like it was nothing. I guess that's what people in L.A. do. I can't wait to get out of here.

Really? Is he just awful?

He was acting all nice and then he showed me around his house and put on the movie that they filmed in Greenville.

I still can't believe he did that. It was like he was trying to upset me after acting so nice. What an asshole.

Is he one of the actors or something?

No, he's the director.

I get out of bed and walk over to the window. The pool is lit up by lights in the sides and bottom. They change from orange to purple as I watch. My phone vibrates.

What? He's Dexter Baldwin?

How the heck does Jess know who he is? The only

reason I had any idea he existed is Mitch was always talking about his movies, but Jess… she doesn't really seem like the action movie type.

Yeah, how did you know?

I'm a HUGE fan.

What? He's an action director….

I watched a ton of action movies with my ex. Plus I have an older brother, so I've been watching Baldwin films for years.

I crack a smile. She's ridiculous. I'm so glad that I can still talk to her. It's bad enough that we don't get to hang out every day. I'm not going to miss the morning runs though, but I'm not about to tell her that.

You're funny.

Yeah, yeah. So what happened?

Well… I kind of ran off, crying, when the movie started playing and locked myself in my room.

It was a little childish, I know, but the emotions that it brought up were just too much. I couldn't help it.

Do you think he was trying to be an ass? Or is he just like that?

I don't know… he seemed so nice at first, so it was weird of him to all of a sudden be an ass. Maybe that's just how people here are. My mom seems so different… it's like I don't even know her anymore.

Not to mention I almost forgot that I need to get out of here and back to Salem.

Crazy. What now? Are you staying there? What about Logan?

I'm only staying here until my birthday and then I'm coming back to Salem. Logan… well things are moving along with him. It was hard to leave him.

Yay! I miss you already! I told you he had the hots for you.

I smile and shake my head. She did tell me that and she was right, even though at the time I thought she was crazy.

I miss you too, I can't wait to get back to Salem so we can hang out again.

I have a feeling that my time here is going to be lonely. I just need to focus on getting a job, making money and getting back to Salem as quickly as possible. That's the only important thing right now. Well... I also need to focus on my relationship with Logan, as much as I can given the distance.

And go for our runs, I miss having you along.

Oh, yes, of course.

It's one of those moments that I wish it were possible to understand sarcasm in a text. I'm totally not missing our runs. Yeah, it was nice to spend time with her and it was good for me to exercise... but getting up so early is awful. I don't miss that at all.

I don't dare mention to Jess that I went on a run the day of my dad's funeral and that it was a good way to clear my head. She would never let me hear the end of it.

One of these days, you are going to realize how amazing morning runs are.

Before I can text Jess back, my phone vibrates again. This time it's a message from Logan.

Can I call you?

I quickly text Jess back.

Can I text you tomorrow? Logan wants to talk on the phone.

Go, talk to your man.

I smile and pull up Logan's number.

"Hey," he says.

"Hi."

"It's good to hear your voice. How are you doing?"

"I'm alright, I guess. How are you?"

"What happened?"

"What do you mean?" I say.

"I can hear it in your voice. You sound upset."

Wow. Am I really that transparent?

"I'm alright."

I don't want to burden Logan with what's happening here. I'm a little worried that if I tell him everything that happens here it won't be good for our relationship in the long term. Plus, I want him to be able to focus on football.

"Amy, I know something is wrong. Please just tell me what it is."

I take a deep breath.

"Well, it turns out that my mom's new boyfriend is Dexter Baldwin. He was the guy that directed the film that was being made in Greenville this year. I guess they must have met then and he basically broke up my family and then you know the rest of the story."

"You told me that you thought it was someone from the crew or one of the actors"

"Yeah, I just didn't think it would be the director. You know?"

"I know what you mean, Baldwin is pretty famous."

I guess I'm the only one who wasn't aware of just how well known he is.

"Which is fine, whatever… I mean I don't get what he could see in her, not now especially."

"What do you mean?"

"She's changed. You talked to her, briefly. She's not my mom anymore as far as I'm concerned. It's like being here has made her a completely different person. She's so… so Hollywood now. I don't get it."

Logan is quiet, but I can tell that he's still there.

"I don't know what to say," he says, finally breaking the silence.

"So that's whatever."

"Is that what upset you?"

"It's part of it. Mostly it's the fact that Baldwin seemed super nice… we had dinner, he showed me around the house… and then he showed me his private theater. Which is fine, but he put on the film from Greenville to show off his theater and it just reminded me… it reminded me of everything that has happened."

"Yeah… that's kind of shitty."

"I mean, he broke up my family. I can never forgive that. I don't care how nice he acts."

"That's fair. I know he hurt you, but do you think that maybe he showed you that movie in an innocent way?"

I wrinkle my forehead. I immediately thought he did it

on purpose to see if he could upset me.

"It's possible that he might have just been excited about his new film and wanted to share that with anyone who would watch it," Logan says.

"I guess so…. I didn't really think of that."

Now I feel bad about running out of the theater. I know what Logan is saying is a possibility, but I also know that Dex could have been doing it on purpose. I just don't know for sure. I should have played it cool, but it's easy to say that now.

"I'm not saying that's what happened, but at least think about it."

"I will."

"Anything else?" Logan says.

"Not really. How was football?"

Logan chuckles.

"What?" I say.

"You're cute."

"Why?"

"Because you asked about football. You're trying to not dominate the conversation."

That was pretty much my exact thought process. We both know that I don't really care all that much about football, but I was trying to be nice.

"I'm glad you think I'm cute."

"You are cute."

I smile. Somehow just talking to Logan can make me feel better about anything.

"You're cute, too." I say.

"I'm cute? Not manly? Or dashing?"

I chuckle. He's ridiculous. He's all of those things and he knows it.

"Just cute."

"Growing up it was my dream to be the cutest boy on my street. I'm glad to see that it came true."

There's a playful tone to his voice. I wish I could see the look on his face right now.

"Well… I don't know if I'd go that far. You're going to have to take me to your hometown and show me the rest of the boys and then I'll decide."

"I guess I might have to take you up on that."

"So," I say, changing the subject, "How was football?"

"It was fine, just a meeting and then I did some physical therapy."

"How's your knee?"

"It's actually getting better, I should be ready to go for the first game of the season."

His voice doesn't falter or crack at all. I'm glad that he seems so confident. I want him to be able to play. When we talked about his knee before I could hear in his voice he wants to be out there with his teammates for summer practice.

"Good. I can't wait to come to a game with Jess."

"I'll score for you."

As cheesy as it sounds, him saying that is really sweet.

"Aww."

Logan laughs.

"That was bad, sorry," he says.

"No, it was cute."

Logan yawns. I think he pulled the phone away, but I still heard it.

"Are you tired?" I say.

"No, I'm fine."

I look at my phone. It's almost one there.

"We should get off the phone, it's really late."

"Ugh. I have a football meeting at seven."

"What? We have to get off the phone right now."

"I feel like we barely talked," he says.

"I know, but tomorrow I'm not doing anything, so whenever you're free we can text or talk again."

Logan sighs. We both know he needs to sleep. I don't want to be responsible for him missing his meeting or falling asleep during it.

"Alright, I'll text you after my meeting."

"Sounds good."

"Dream about me," he says.

He ends the call before I can respond.

I hope that I do dream about him.

CHAPTER FIVE

A faint knock on my door wakes me up. I look over at the clock and blink. It says nine, but there's no way it can be right. I never sleep this late.

There's a second knock on my door.

Part of me really wants to pretend like I don't hear it. It's probably my mom or maybe even Dex and I have no desire to see either of them.

Whoever it is knocks on my door a third time. I groan and sit up in bed. I wrap the sheet around myself and walk to the door. I put a dirty look on my face and open it.

My eyes meet Gina's and I quickly smile. I can tell it's too late, she has a mortified look on her face.

"Sorry, Miss Amy. Did I wake you?"

"No, it's fine, I was already awake."

A twinge of guilt passes through my body. I feel bad for giving her such a dirty look.

"Would you like some breakfast."

I almost say no, but my stomach grumbles loud enough for her to hear it and she smiles.

"Come down whenever you're ready."

Gina turns and walks back downstairs. I close the door and go to the closet to find something to throw on. I put on a T-shirt and pajama bottoms and head downstairs.

The table is set for one and I sit down. Gina brings over a plate of food and sets it in front of me.

"Would you like some milk or juice?"

"Juice, please."

Gina nods and heads to the fridge. I look down at the amazing breakfast that she set in front of me. There's two strips of bacon, a fried egg, some wheat toast and sliced apple. It looks really good.

"Do you need anything else?" she says, as she sets down a glass of orange juice in front of me.

"No, this is amazing, Gina. Thank you."

"Of course, Miss Amy. I'll just be cleaning up if you need anything else."

I nod and reach for the orange juice. The moment it touches my lips I can tell it's fresh squeezed. It's the best orange juice I've ever had. I set the glass down and turn to Gina, who is already at the sink washing some dishes.

"Gina?"

She turns and starts walking toward me. I hold up my hands.

"Sorry, it's not that important. I was just wondering if my mom or Dex are around."

I actually don't care, it's not like I want to talk to them, but I'm trying to figure out what I'll need to do to avoid them. If I can help it, I'll be out of here and looking for a job within the next hour.

"Mr. Baldwin left already, he said he would probably be late, and Ms. K went out of town this morning. Ricardo drove her and Mr. Baldwin said that if you needed to go somewhere, to just let me know and I can call a limo service for you."

"Thanks."

She nods and turns back to her cleaning.

Weird. I wonder where my mom went. Not that I really care, but still. And a limo? There's no way I can, or want, to take a limo out on a job hunt. That would just be ridiculous and potential employers wouldn't take me seriously if they saw me pull up.

I take a bite of the egg, which is cooked perfectly and follow it with a bite of bacon. It's amazing how good all the food tastes. This is something I could get used to. I'm definitely going to miss Gina's cooking when I leave.

When we were driving here yesterday, I did notice some businesses that weren't too far away. I'm not sure exactly what they were, but I figure that's the best place for me to start looking.

I finish the orange juice and most of my breakfast, only leaving a few bites of egg, and stand up from the table.

"Was everything OK?"

"It was great, Gina, thank you so much."

"Did you want me to call a limo for you?"

"No, it's alright," I say, shaking my head.

"OK, Miss Amy, let me know if you change your mind. If you want lunch, I'll be around and dinner should be at seven."

I smile at her and nod. She's sweet. I'm glad that I get to talk to her, she seems like the only genuine one around here. She smiles at me and turns back to her cleaning.

I walk back upstairs and take a deep breath once I close and lock my door. I don't know how I'm going to make it until my birthday. It isn't going to be easy, that's for sure.

~~~

I stand in front of the floor length mirror and look at myself. I like my outfit, I think it's cute. I'm wearing a pair of jeans, a white scoop neck sweater with pink stripes and black sneakers.

I grab my phone and check to see if I have any messages from Logan or from Jess. I'm a little disappointed when I don't see anything from either of them. I put my phone in my purse and put it over my shoulder.

I take a deep breath. You can do this, Amy, you'll get a job and in no time you can save enough money to go back to Salem after your birthday.

Gina isn't in the kitchen when I walk through on my way to the front door.

"Gina?"

I call out for her, but there's no response. I wanted to tell her I was leaving, just so that no one wondered where I was. I don't know why I care, it's not like my mom would even care if I was gone when she got home.

The front door is locked, which seems a little strange to me since there's a gate and a fence around the whole property. I don't have a key, so hopefully someone is here when I get back. I lock the handle of the door and close it behind me.

When I get close to the gate, maybe ten feet away, it opens automatically. I walk to the sidewalk and turn around to make sure the gate closes. Once it's all the way closed, I turn toward Santa Monica Boulevard. I figure that's where I'll have the best shot at getting a job.

It's amazing how busy the road is. There's cars everywhere, people walking up and down the streets. It's all a little overwhelming.

It's kind of funny, I thought that Salem was busy and crowded... but now... now I see what a real city is like.

There are shops on both sides of the streets, so it shouldn't be too hard for me to find one that's hiring. I continue down the side that I'm already on. The first few places are closed, but after a couple of minutes I come across a local coffee shop and head inside.

The smell of coffee fills my nose. It's a wonderful smell. I don't really like drinking coffee, but the smell is divine. There's a line, almost to the door, so I wait my turn. When it's my turn, the girl behind the counter flashes me a huge smile.

"What can I get started for you?"

"Actually, I was wondering if you were hiring?"

Her smile fades and she rolls her eyes.

"Let me get my manager."

She walks away and taps the shoulder of a guy who's using the espresso machine. He glances over his shoulder at me and nods to the girl. She walks back over to me and gives me a dirty look.

"Take a seat and he'll come talk to you."

Sheesh, I wonder what her problem is. I walk over to an empty table and sit down. I take my phone out of my purse, but there's still no text from Logan. He must be busy with football. Hopefully he's free later, I really want to talk to him.

I can't believe it's been twenty-four hours since I felt Logan's lips on mine. It feels like a lifetime ago.

"Hi."

I look up and see the manager sitting down across from me. His name tag says he's Ted. I quickly throw my phone back in my purse and turn my attention to him.

"Hello, I'm Amy."

"Amy, I'm Ted. Nice to meet you."

"You too."

"So, you're looking for a job?"

"Yes."

"What's your barista experience like?"

"I don't have any."

He frowns at me. I didn't even think about that before walking in here. I just assumed that places like this would be willing to train people. By the look on his face I can tell that I was mistaken.

"Hmm… well… do you have a résumé?"

I hadn't thought of that either. I know it's standard to have one when applying for most jobs, but I didn't think that it was necessary for a job like this.

"No."

He glares at me as if I'm just wasting his time.

"Well," he says, standing up, "If you get one, bring it in."

He walks away as I stand up. I feel the eyes of everyone on me. I hurry out of the coffee shop and keep on walking.

That was such a weird feeling. I don't like the fact that I felt like I was being judged by Ted, the guy is just a manager of a coffee shop, when I didn't do anything wrong.

I should figure out a way to get my résumé written, I just didn't see a computer at the house. I guess I might need to find a library. There must be one somewhere around here.

I feel a little defeated, after the coffee shop, but I'm not about to give up. My desire to get out of here is too strong.

There are two restaurants farther down the street, but they are both still closed. I guess I should have waited until later in the day to go job hunting. I keep walking until I come across a boutique clothing store that is just opening. I guess it's worth a shot. How hard can selling clothes be?

I walk into the clothing store and glance around. Everything looks expensive. The store even smells expensive. I see two girls working behind the sales counter near the back and I walk toward them. As I get closer, one turns to the other and whispers something and they both start to giggle.

When I reach the counter, they both give me disinterested looks and continue folding shirts.

"Hi, I was wondering if…."

"Our bathroom is for customers only," the one on the left says.

Weird. I wonder why she thought I was looking for a bathroom.

"I wasn't looking for a bathroom. I was actually wondering if you were hiring?"

They look at each other and then back to me and start laughing. I'm not sure what's so funny. I'm starting to regret coming in here, these two girls are acting so weird.

"Are you serious?" the right one says.

I feel like for the second time already this morning people are talking to me like I'm stupid. I can feel rage building inside my body and I know that I need to walk out of here right now.

Without saying anything to them, I turn around and start walking toward the front door.

"Can you believe her? Wearing *that* and coming in here asking for a job. What a joke."

I stop. I know she said it loud enough for me to hear. I really want to say something. I take a deep breath and keep walking and they start laughing. I keep my head down and walk out the door.

The more I think about what just happened, the angrier I get. Why would they say something so mean? I thought that my outfit today looked really cute. Yeah, it wasn't expensive like the clothes in that store, but that doesn't mean it can't look nice.

I clench my teeth and turn toward home. That's as much as I can take for one day. I need to get a résumé and try some of the restaurants tomorrow. I should have better luck with them since I have experience.

I'm not giving up, not yet. I need to get out of here. I'm just going home to try and figure out where I can write a résumé. Maybe Gina knows of where there is a computer I can use.

I force myself to be strong as I walk home. It's just a setback, Amy, you're better than those girls or the manager of a coffee shop, you can do anything.

CHAPTER SIX

I feel a little calmer by the time I get back to the house, but I'm still upset about what happened. I just can't believe that people can treat other people like that. Is it L.A.? So far Gina is the only kind person I've met. She must not be from here.

I walk up to the gate, forgetting that I didn't have any way to get back inside. That was kind of stupid of me. I see a button and what looks like a speaker. I press the button and wait.

"Yes?"

It's Gina. Hearing her voice makes me feel a little better about everything.

"Gina, it's Amy. Can you let me in please?"

"Sure, Miss Amy, just one second."

The gate buzzes and then swings open. I walk through and it closes behind me. When I reach the front door, Gina has it open and is waiting for me.

"Where did you go Miss Amy?"

I walk inside and she closes the door behind me.

"I went to go look for a job."

"You walked?"

I nod. I don't mind walking really, I've spent so many

years getting around that way. I always do my best thinking while I walk, too.

"You didn't want me to call a limo for you?"

I shake my head and walk into the kitchen. Gina follows me and while I'm searching the cupboards for a glass, she opens the fridge and pulls out a bottle of water for me.

"Thanks."

"You looked thirsty."

I open the bottle and drink half of it.

"Is everything OK?"

I want to tell someone what happened today, but her job isn't listening to me complain. I'm sure that Gina has much better things to do.

"Yep, everything is fine."

I feel bad about not telling her what's wrong. She's been so nice.

"OK, well if you need anything, just let me know. And if you want to go out again, please let me call a car for you. Mr. Baldwin would be upset if I let you walk around town, alone."

Her voice sounds shaky. I wrinkle my brow as she turns away. He would be upset at her? She's not my nanny or anything. So strange.

"Oh, Gina."

She turns around from the sink.

"Do you know where there's a public library or something? I need to use a computer."

"Mr. Baldwin has a home office, I'm sure it would be fine if you wanted to use his computer."

"You don't think he would mind?"

"Not at all," she says, shaking her head.

I really would rather not use his computer, but I don't really see much of an alternative. I'm not going to take a limo to a library and it sounds like Gina could get in trouble with Dex if I leave on foot. I don't want to jeopardize her relationship with Dex. If she got fired because of me, I would never forgive myself.

"Alright, where is his office?"

"Follow me, I'll show you."

We head up the staircase by the front door and we go into the first room on the right, just across the hall from the master bedroom.

The room is even bigger than my bedroom. There is a massive TV along one wall and a desk in the center of the room. On the desk is a large computer monitor and a printer next to it. Everything in the room looks brand new. I wonder if this is another one of the rooms that Dex never goes in, especially since he didn't show it to me during the tour.

"Are you sure it's OK that I use his computer?"

"Yes, it's fine. He almost never uses this room."

She smiles at me and leaves the room. I shrug. I guess I'm using his computer without his permission. I hope he doesn't get mad, but I guess if Gina says it's OK then it must be.

I set my purse on the floor, sit down at the desk and hit the power button on the computer. I look around the room while I wait for it to start up. There are movie posters on the walls, a far cry from the art in the rest of the house. Most of them look like they are from action movies, which means they're probably the posters from movies that Dex directed.

The screen comes on as the computer finishes starting up. There is the usual assortment of icons on the desktop, mostly programs, organized into neat rows on the left side... but on the right side there are a couple of folders. One is named pictures and the other is new folder.

I wonder what's inside the folders? I move the mouse pointer over the one that says new folder. Should I look? I'm not really a snoopy person, but I don't really know anything about Dex and he did ruin my family.

I can't believe I'm trying to justify looking at Dex's private things that are on his personal computer. Well... if he wanted to keep it private, wouldn't he have put a password on the computer?

No. That's not me. I don't care how much of an ass he was to me, I'm not going to snoop through his private things. I move the cursor away and open the word processing program.

My phone, still in my purse on the floor, chirps. I pull it out and see a message from Logan waiting for me.

Hey. Sorry it took so long, I just got done with physical therapy.

I crack a smile. Just seeing the text from him is already making feel better after what happened today.

It's all good, I figured that you were just busy. How is your knee?

My knee is good. I'll be ready for the start of the season. How are you?

Where to start? I know he's trying to focus on football right now. I feel bad about complaining about my day when I'm sure he's already had a hard day and it's not over.

I'm fine, how are you?

I don't like bending the truth, especially with Logan... but I just can't stress him out. It's already hard enough for both of us that we have to be apart that I don't want to put any more pressure on him.

Really? You're doing alright?

It's like he already knows me well enough that he can tell that something is wrong.

I'm OK, I guess. It's not a big deal, I can deal with it.

I feel better now that I told him the truth. I can deal with it and I plan on doing just that. The coffee shop and the girls in the clothing store were just a minor setback and tomorrow I will find a job. I don't really have a choice, not if I want to get out of here as soon as possible and get back to Logan, and Salem.

Are you sure? Do you want to at least talk about it?

I take a deep breath. I know that he might be able to help me feel a little better, but he can't fix my problems for me. Especially not from thousands of miles away.

It's fine. I don't want to bother you when you are trying to focus on football, I know how important it is.

I feel a pang of guilt. I should have listened to myself and not brought it up in the first place. Now I'm going to have to tell Logan what happened today or he's going to be worried about me.

Amy, if we are really going to do this we have to be able to talk about anything. If there's something bothering you, you should feel like you can tell me about it.

He's amazing. It's what every girl wants to hear, but never expects they will. A smile forms on my face. I wish I could kiss him right now.

You're so sweet.

I'm serious. If there's anything, and I mean anything, that you want to tell me or talk to me about, you should. I'm here for you.

Well, today I went to look for a job. The first place, the manager wanted a résumé and wanted to know what kind of barista experience I had. The second place was a clothing store, and the girls working there laughed me out of the store and made fun of my outfit.

Talking about it makes me want to cry. How can people be so mean? Those girls don't even know me.

Forget those girls, they were probably just jealous.

I laugh out loud.

Jealous?

Yeah, you have a really cute boyfriend. Plus, you're an amazing girl and you're beautiful on top of it.

I crack a smile and laugh again. He's absurd. I love it. I wish that every moment could be like this. Well… I wish that I was with Logan, but other than that it seems perfect.

Thank you, you're sweet. And yes, I do have a cute boyfriend.

So, maybe you should try getting a résumé written or you can try somewhere else. Where are you now?

Before I can respond there's a knock on the frame of the door. I look up and see Gina standing in the doorway with a plate in her hand.

"I brought you some food, Miss Amy."

She walks into the room and sets a plate down on the

desk.

"Thank you."

Gina smiles, turns and walks back out of the room. I look down at a grilled cheese sandwich that is cooked to perfection. The edges are just turning brown and the cheese is oozing out of the sides. I can see the steam rising off it and decide to text Logan while it cools down.

I'm back at the house now. I'm in the office getting ready to write a résumé.

Do you want me to stop bugging you so that you can get it done?

No, it's not going anywhere. I'm not doing anything else today. I'm going to go out tomorrow and try again to find a job.

I pick up the sandwich and take a bite. My suspicions are confirmed. It's amazing and cooked to perfection. I used to think my mom made the best grilled cheese, but this puts hers to shame.

Have you talked to your mom since you got there?

No, she went out with friends after we got here and she was gone when I got up this morning.

I take another bite of the sandwich, finishing one of the triangle halves. It's so delicious, I never want it to end. I need to be careful, with the way Gina cooks I might start eating and never stop.

Weird. Did she go out a lot with friends when you lived in Greenville?

No, she was home every night and we ate dinner as a family. She's a completely different person. There's really nothing about her that is reminiscent of her old life.

A minute goes by without a response from Logan, so turn my attention back to the computer. The word processing program is open and asking what kind of document I want to create. I spot an option for a résumé and select it and then select the first template. A basic resume with filler pops onto the screen. It looks like I can just fill in my information and it will be all set. My phone chirps with a text from Logan.

Sorry about that, coach stopped by my room.

Is everything OK?

I scan the top of the résumé template. I frown at the top line. I have no idea of the address here. I guess I'll just fill in the rest and ask Gina for that.

Yeah, it's fine. He just wanted an update on my knee. So, where did your mom go this morning?

I have no idea, Gina said that Ricardo took my mom and she didn't say when she was coming back.

I finish the last bite of the grilled cheese. I'm actually a little sad to be finished with it.

Who's Gina and Ricardo?

I guess I never mentioned them to Logan, it didn't seem very important.

Gina is the cook and maybe housekeeper, I'm not really sure of what all she does around here. Ricardo is the driver, he picked us up from the airport.

Wow, living like a rock star. Are you sure you want to come back to Salem? It's not nearly as exciting. I mean, I'll drive you around, but I'm not a very good cook or housekeeper.

Yes, I'm sure I want to go back to Salem. You can't leave me hanging with just one kiss.

I fill out my name and phone number before my phone chimes.

Two kisses. Don't forget the vomit kiss. I know I won't.

Ugh. I'm glad he can't see my face right now because I'm mortified. I still can't believe I did that. I'm not drinking again for a long time, that's for sure.

I was hoping you forgot. I still feel bad about that.

It's all good, I'm just teasing you. It was certainly a first kiss that I'll never forget and that's a good thing.

Now that I think about it, he's right, it makes for a silly memory. Who knows, I might even get over the sheer humiliation one of these days and it could be a funny story to tell people.

I won't forget it either.

Gina knocks on the door frame again and I look up from my phone.

"Was your sandwich OK?"

"It was wonderful, thank you."

She walks over to the table, picks up the plate and turns around.

"Wait, I almost forgot," I say.

Gina turns back around and smiles at me.

"I'm writing a résumé and I don't know the address here."

She looks at me for a moment as if she's trying to figure something out. She finally nods, walks back to the desk and sets down the plate, and she grabs a pen from the desk and writes the address down on a scrap piece of paper.

"Thank you."

"You should ask Mr. Baldwin before you hand that out. If people find out where he lives… well, I don't think he would be all that happy."

It's something I had never even thought about. I wonder what that must be like. I guess I need to be careful with who I talk to in this city. Every minute more I spend here, the less I like it here.

"Alright, thank you."

She smiles and walks out of the room. I'm not looking forward to talking to Dex about this or anything, I'm still mad at him.

I fill in the address and quickly read through it to make sure it all looks correct. My phone chirps as I hit print on the document. The printer comes to life as I check my phone.

I hope we have many more moments together that we don't soon forget.

Aww. He's so sweet.

Me too.

I grab my résumé from the printer, give it a quick glance to make sure that everything is OK, and shut down Dex's computer and leave the room, closing the door behind myself.

CHAPTER SEVEN

There's a faint knock on my door and I set my phone down on the bed. I'm sure it's Gina, she always knocks softly. I open my bedroom door and smile at Gina.

"Miss Amy, I just wanted to let you know that Mr. Baldwin will be home in ten minutes or so and he would like you to join him for dinner."

I try not to frown, but I'm not sure it works because I can see in her face that's she's confused. She smiles at me and walks away.

Gina has no idea what Dex did to my family and what he did to me by showing me the film of Greenville. I get the impression that she has a great deal of respect for him. I have a feeling that she might be naive enough to not be upset by the way Hollywood people act. It's actually a little surprising considering what she does for a living. Maybe she sees it and doesn't mind.

I sit back down on my bed and pick up my phone. There's a message waiting for me, from Logan.

I should probably get going, I have a team dinner and then we have a late film study session.

It's really amazing how much time he's putting into football, considering the season hasn't even started yet.

OK, thanks for listening. Have a good night, I'll talk to you tomorrow.

I wait for a minute, but don't get a reply. He must already be at his team dinner.

My mind drifts back to Dex. I wonder why he wants me to join him for dinner. After last night, I'm surprised that he even wants to talk to me… unless he wants to remind me again how he ruined my family. I hope that's not the case, because if that's what he has in mind I'm not sticking around.

I look at my phone and wonder why I haven't heard from Jess today. She must be busy or maybe she had to work all day. Hopefully, she'll text me when she gets home from work.

While I wait for Dex to get home, I scroll through my phone and eventually open up my voicemails. There are three messages from my dad that I just can't bring myself to listen to, again. I know the sound of his voice, even though he was pissed at me in the voicemails, will instantly make me cry and hate my current situation even more.

I keep wondering if Dex is to blame for all of this. If he hadn't come to make his movie, then my mom wouldn't have left; my dad would have never started drinking so heavily and I would have never left home. He would never have had to come see me in Salem and would still be alive today.

I know it's a lot of *what if's*, but there's a part of me that can't stop from feeling that way.

I sigh, sensing that close to ten minutes has gone by since Gina knocked on my door. I get up and head downstairs. The sooner I get down there and dinner starts, the sooner I don't have to look at his face.

When I walk into the kitchen Gina is standing over the stove. I sit down at the table, at my same spot, and notice that it's set for three. I groan. The spot between Dex and me is set. It can only mean that my mom is going to be here, which I'm definitely not looking forward to.

I feel my phone vibrate in my pocket and I pull it out. A smile crosses my face as I see the text from Jess.

Hey, girly, I just got home from work. How's it going today? Did you tell your mom off yet?

Lol. No, I actually haven't seen her yet. I guess I will in a second though, Dex asked for me to have dinner with him and I'm sitting at the table waiting for him right now and there's a third spot set. Here goes nothing.

Don't hold back. Tell them what they did to you.

That would be nice. I would love to tell Dex he ruined my family and that he's an awful person for it. I want to tell my mom that I never want to see or speak to her again, I just don't know if I have it in me. If they push me, though, I'm sure that I'll let them know exactly how much I hate them.

I hear laughing and I set my phone down on the table and look up. Dex walks through the door and sits down. My mouth drops open when I see the other person with him. It's not my mother, but instead a strikingly handsome guy who looks to be in his early twenties.

He looks so familiar. He must just have one of those faces.

"This is Amy," Dex says, as they sit down.

"Nice to meet you, Amy, I'm Spencer."

Holy crap. That's why I recognize him.

"As in Spencer Thomas?" I say.

He smiles and nods.

"I cast him in my next movie," Dex says.

I still can't believe it. He's a genuine movie star, a heartthrob... one of those boys that all the girls in high school had a picture of in their locker. I never thought he was *that* good looking, but sitting just a few feet away from him right now... I can see why he has that image. Even though he's good looking, when I look at him I don't feel the same way I feel when I look at Logan.

"Amy."

"Huh?"

I blink and look at Dex. I guess I was lost in my own world.

"I told Spencer that you're going to school in Salem this fall."

I nod. That's the plan, so long as you don't ruin that for me, too.

"Are you a football fan?"

I shrug. I guess? How do I answer that?

"Oh… well, my dad went to State so I grew up a Cougar fan," Spencer says.

"I didn't know that," Dex says.

"Yeah. I'm looking forward to this season, they have a good shot at winning their conference if their quarterback comes back from his knee injury."

Knee injury? Is Logan the starting quarterback? I hadn't even considered it. Is that why the guy in the restaurant, when I went out with Logan the day I met him, recognized him?

"What's his name?" I say.

"Logan Reynolds."

I can't believe it. That must be why Mitch was so suspicious of me and Logan. He thought that I was going after the quarterback of the team. Suddenly things start to make sense. That's why Logan is always going to meetings and football is such an important part of his life. I feel bad about complaining about my problems all the time when he has the weight of a football team on his shoulders.

"You alright, Amy? You look… surprised," Dex says.

I nod my head. He's right, I'm surprised. How come Logan never mentioned it before?

"You know him, don't you?" Spencer says.

I turn my head toward him and look him in the eyes. I think about not saying anything, it's the smart thing to do. I don't want my mom or Dex to have anything they can hold over my head. They don't need to know anything about me or my life. At the same time, Spencer has a sheer look of joy on his face.

"Yeah… I know him."

"Eeee!"

I smile at Spencer. I've never heard a guy squeal like that before. It's endearing and it makes him seem more… normal.

"Do you…. Oh, never mind. I'm sure it's not possible."

"What is it?"

"Do you think you could get me an autograph? Do you know him well enough to ask for one?"

"You could say that."

He has a huge smile on his face. Spencer Thomas, famous actor, looks like a kid in a candy store. How could I say no?

"Thank you, so much!"

"No problem."

I grab my phone to text Logan. I know he's probably busy, but I want to do it before I forget.

Spencer Thomas, the actor, is at the house right now. He's a huge fan, his dad is an alumni of State. He was wondering if you could sign an autograph for him.

I hit send and put my phone back down.

"Wait… did you just text *him*?" Spencer says.

"Yeah… why?"

"You have his phone number?"

"Yeah."

"That's amazing. How did you meet him?"

I almost blurt out that I walked in on him in the bathroom, with just a towel wrapped around him. I'm glad that I don't. That's not a story I really want to be telling people. I try to think of a way that I can say we met that doesn't involve a bathroom or Mitch.

"We met… at my old job. I worked at a place called Burgers-R-Us."

It's a little bit of a white lie, but Logan *did* come into my work and that was a link in the chain of events that led to us being together.

51

"Crazy... you never know."

I look over at Dex, who has been silent the whole time. He has a smile on his face and I can tell he's getting a kick out of this.

"Are you and Logan...." Spencer says.

"That's enough, Spencer," Dex says. "Let the poor girl be."

Gina sets a plate down in front of me and I'm thankful for her, and Dex's interruption. I don't mind talking to Spencer, but I don't really know much about Logan when it comes to football, obviously, so it was starting to go in a direction I didn't feel comfortable talking about. Not to mention Logan and I are still getting to know each other.

"Sorry," Spencer says.

"It's fine, no worries. I'll let you know when I hear back from him."

He looks up from his plate and smiles at me. I wonder how many girls would give anything in the world to be sitting at a table with Spencer Thomas smiling at them. Granted it's because I know Logan, but still.

My phone vibrates. It surprises me as I figure Logan is going to be busy all night. When I pick it up there isn't a message from Logan, but instead a message from my provider.

Dear Customer, your service has been terminated for non-payment. Please call or make a payment online to have your service turned back on. Thanks.

"Is that from Logan?" Spencer says.

I shake my head and read the message again. What the heck?

Then it comes to me. I'm sure my dad was the one paying the cell phone bill. I guess I should have known that this would happen at some point, just not this soon. Now... now I don't know what I'm going to do.

"Is everything OK?" Dex says.

"I guess so... my phone just got shut off."

A thousand thoughts go through my head. How am I

going to afford a phone without a job? How will jobs I apply for get ahold of me? I guess I can't text Logan or Jess.

Ugh. This sucks. I need to figure something out, fast.

"I can get you a phone, that's not a big deal, don't worry about it," Dex says.

The last thing I want is for him to help me.

"That's alright, I'll figure it out."

A surprised look crosses his face. Dex turns his attention to the burger in front of him. I look down at my food for the first time. There's a burger on my plate, in a sesame seed bun with lettuce, tomato and onion. There are fries on the side and Gina has also put a glass of water in front of me. I feel bad, I was so absorbed by everything that I didn't get a chance to thank her.

I pick up my burger and take a bite. It's amazing. Everything tastes so fresh and clean. I set it down and eat two of the fries. They are salty and delicious. Hands down the best fries I've ever had.

Gina walks over to the table and scans it to make sure that everyone has what they need. I catch her gaze and I smile at her.

"Is everything OK?" Gina says.

"Yeah, it's wonderful," I say.

"It's good, thanks Gina." Dex says.

Spencer says something through a mouthful of burger, but I don't think any of us were able to decipher it.

Dex laughs at Spencer. It's something that I would probably laugh at usually, but tonight... I just don't feel like laughing. I don't like that I'm sad, but I know that once I'm back in Salem with Logan things will be better and I'll be back to my old self... back to how I was before Dex showed up in Greenville.

I feel sick. Not from the food, but from having to be here.

"Excuse me, I'm not feeling well."

I stand up from the table and walk out. I head upstairs

to my room and plop down on the bed. I look at my phone, expecting the *No Service* text to disappear from the top left of the screen by some magic. I wish.

~~~

There is a knock on my door, harder than Gina's but still not very hard. I groan. It's probably my mom. The last thing I need after the day I've had is a confrontation with her.

I walk over to the door, take a deep breath and pull it open. Standing in front of me with a worried look on his face is Dex.

"Are you alright?" he says.

"Yeah, I'm fine. What do you need?"

"Can I talk to you?"

"We are talking."

He takes a deep breath. He looks worried. What could someone like him, a rich wife stealer, ever be worried about? Rich people don't have problems. Not problems like I have anyway. If anything, they cause them.

"No, I want to sit down with you and have a conversation, like adults."

I don't know what he could possibly have to say to me that I would want to hear. I have nothing to say to him. I close the door in his face. I don't owe him a damn thing.

I sit down on my bed and put my head in my hands and start to cry. I think I hear a soft knock on the door, but I don't even bother checking to see who it is or what they want.

CHAPTER EIGHT

I look over at the clock, again. Eleven in the morning and I still don't feel like getting out of bed. There's no reason.

There was a soft knock on my door earlier, sometime around nine, which I assume was Gina telling me that breakfast was ready, but I didn't even bother getting up. I just closed my eyes and tried to go back to sleep.

After the failed job search yesterday, I was planning to go back to that coffee shop with my résumé and scout out a couple more places that might be hiring.

When my phone got shut off, I completely lost all desire to do anything. I feel lost. I can't talk to Logan or Jess and it's killing me.

I check my phone again, for probably the fifth time this morning and still no service. I'm not sure what to do really.

There's a light knock on the door and I lift my head. It's Gina and even though she has been the nicest person since I got here... I don't think I can face her. I feel too crappy and depressed.

I hear the doorknob turning. I know that I locked it,

but as I peek from behind the covers I can see that it's not stopping Gina. She pushes the door open, picks a tray up off the floor and walks toward the bed.

"Miss Amy, you can't just stay in here forever."

I'm still baffled as to how she got the door open.

"You need to eat something and you'll feel better."

I sit up in bed and prop the pillow against the headboard, behind my back. Gina sets the tray over my legs and pulls the silver top off. There is a plate of plain wheat toast, some grapes and a steaming bowl of soup.

"My mother's chicken noodle soup. It will cure anything."

I raise my eyebrows at her. It won't cure my blues.

"Anything. You eat it and tell me that it doesn't help."

She turns and walks toward the door.

"Gina, thank you."

She turns around and smiles at me.

"Just doing my job."

"No, Gina. Thank you for everything. Since I left Salem everything has been… hard. And you're the only nice person I've met since leaving and it means the world to me."

She walks back over to the bed and stands at the foot and looks into my eyes.

"You're a special girl. I can tell you'll do great things, but you've had a lot of tragedy in your life. They're just setbacks and they will make you the woman you are destined to be."

I nod my head. I hope she's right. I hope that I'm stronger from all of this, but I'm also so ready for it to be done with. I just want to be happy. I just want Logan to hold me in his arms and kiss me. That's it. Is that too much to ask?

"That's very kind of you."

"I'm just telling you the truth," she says, shrugging. "And I know I'm not the *only* nice person you've met since you got here. You know Mr. Baldwin and he's one of the nicest people I've ever met."

I wrinkle my nose and turn my attention to the food in front of me. I'm not really hungry, but I don't think I can look at Gina right now. I'm sure she would be able to tell that I'm not exactly fond of Dex.

"Miss Amy, what's wrong?"

I shake my head. I can't tell her, not after what she just said about Dex. If I tell her my side of the story, she would probably tell him and then who knows… anything could happen. He knows I'm stuck here, for now, and if he really wanted to he could make my life even more miserable.

"It's OK," she says, as she sits on the end of the bed. "You can tell me anything. I won't say anything to anyone."

There's truth in her voice. I just don't know though. When I look into her eyes, I can see that I can trust her. I'm not sure why I'm being so resistant. I shouldn't care if Dex finds out. He can't do anything to me.

"You won't tell Dex or my mom?"

She shakes her head, puts her hand on my foot and squeezes it.

"I won't say anything."

I take a bite of the toast as I think about what to tell her and how I should say it. I don't want to be unkind about Dex, even though he was an ass to me, because she seems to think he's a great guy.

"I… it's just been hard."

I pop a grape into my mouth and look up at Gina. She has a look of motherly understanding on her face.

"I didn't want to come here, I really didn't. I have a new boyfriend, a guy that I'm crazy about and I had to leave him."

Gina has a confused look on her face.

"Why did you come? I assumed you wanted to come here."

I shake my head. I wonder where she got that impression.

"My dad died and since I'm not quite eighteen, my mom made me come here. I didn't have any choice at all."

A look of surprise crosses her face. I find it hard to believe that anyone would be here by choice.

"A lot of girls your age would be so excited to be in Hollywood, living in a mansion."

I nod. She's right, but not me.

"Yeah, I'm sure they would. I'm just not one of them. I hate it here. I hate how mean everyone is. I just want to be back in Salem with Logan."

Gina squeezes my foot and smiles at me.

"How long will you be here?"

"Only as long as I have to be."

I don't feel like getting into needing to get a job and make money so that I can get the hell out of here. Not to mention I've gotta get a new phone. I'll never make it until my birthday if I can't talk to Logan or Jess.

"Well, if there's anything I can do to help your time here be a little... easier just let me know."

"Thank you, Gina. You've been so kind. You're the only person here I actually like."

There's a brief flash of disappointment on her face. She pushes the feeling away and forces a smile. I can tell she doesn't understand how I don't feel the same way about Dex as she does.

"No problem."

She gets up and walks toward the door.

"Wait," I say. "Is there a phone here?"

"No, there's not. Mr. Baldwin always just uses his cell."

"Alright, thanks."

She walks out of the room and pulls the door closed. I wanted to call Logan and tell him that my phone got shut off. He's probably already texted me this morning and is wondering why I haven't texted him back.

I can't breathe. I jump out of bed, push the window and stick my head outside. I take a deep breath, but it doesn't seem to help. I need Logan. I need him to hold me in his arms and tell me that it's going to be OK.

I grab the bottle of water off my nightstand and drink the rest of it in one swallow. I sit down on the bed and try to slow my breathing.

I feel like my world is still falling apart around me. I thought it was over, the moment I buried my dad, but it just keeps getting worse. When will it be over?

Is this what my life is going to be like? I can't live like this.

Something has got to change. It's impossible for me to just sit in my room until my birthday. I need to get a job and make some money, that's the most important thing.

I take one last deep breath as my pulse slows. I don't feel right. It's not like I'm sick or anything… I'm not sure what it is exactly. I just feel sad. Like really sad. It's almost impossible to describe. Ugh.

I grab my purse off the shelf in my room and sit back down on the bed. I pull out my wallet and start counting my money. One hundred and twenty-seven dollars. I was hoping it would be a little more, maybe enough to get a bus ticket back to Salem. I sigh and put the money back and put my wallet in my purse.

I run my hand through my hair as I try to figure out what I'm going to do. I need a job. The main problem is I can't hand out a résumé with a disconnected phone number. I guess first things first, I need a phone.

Get yourself together, Amy, you can do this. Go get a phone and go get a job.

I throw on the same clothes I wore yesterday, since I didn't exactly do much, and head out of my room.

I sneak down the front stairs, listening to see if

Gina is around. The house seems silent, so I quietly open the front door and close it behind me.

Gina mentioned that she didn't want me leaving on foot, and neither did Dex, but I don't really care. I know he wants to get me out of his house as soon as possible, so I'm going to try and make that happen.

I glance back at the front door as the gate opens, half expecting to see Gina come running out. When she doesn't, I turn and start walking toward Santa Monica Boulevard.

When I get there, I cross at the first intersection and head in the opposite direction from yesterday. I don't want to walk by the coffee shop or the store with the girls, plus I need to find a phone.

After a couple of blocks I see a store for my wireless provider. I open the door and go inside. A man with a clipboard walks over to me and smiles.

"Hi, do you have an appointment?"

I frown and look around. There's only two customers and three people working. Is he serious?

"No."

He looks down at the clipboard and scans the sheet of paper.

"OK, it should only be a five or ten minute wait if you want to take a seat."

He points at a chair near the door. I glare at him, but he's already walking away. Seriously? Why would I think I needed an appointment?

I go and sit in the chair. This is what's wrong with cell phone providers. So stupid.

A few minutes pass before one of the salesmen comes over to me with a smug look on his face.

"How can I help you today? We just got in a shipment of Smartphones in this morning. Are you looking to upgrade?"

I shake my head as I stand up. A defeated look crosses his face before the smile takes its place again. I guess he really wanted to sell an expensive phone with a plan to match.

"My service got shut off, so I was wondering how much it would be for just a basic phone."

He nods slowly as if he was racking his brain to try and think of the best way to separate me from my money.

"Well... I can check your account and see how much it would cost to get your phone turned back on."

I perk up. I don't know why I didn't think of that. If it's not too expensive that would solve all of my problems. I could keep my phone, which I'm still in love with, and not have to transfer anything.

"That would be great, thanks."

"Just come with me and I'll pull up your account."

I follow him over to the counter. He walks around the end and starts to pound away on a computer. He finally looks up at me.

"If you could enter your phone number into the pin pad."

I put my number in and press enter. He stares at the screen for what feels like forever and then he cringes, looks at me and looks back to the screen.

"Well... it's not good."

"What's not?"

"Your account."

He doesn't say anything else. I guess he wants me to read his mind.

"OK... what's so bad about it?"

He stares at me and then looks back to the screen, moving his lips as he reads. How does this guy have a job and I don't?

"It looks like you are two months behind on payments... so you would have to pay those, the late fees and the fee to turn it back on again."

He looks at me, as if waiting for me to say something.

"How much is it?"

He blinks and keeps looking at me.

"For what?" he says.

I want to scream. Is this why they charge so much money for their crappy service? So they can afford to hire mental giants like this guy?

"How much would it be to pay it all… to get my phone turned back on?"

"Right, let me just check."

What the heck has he been doing this whole time?

"It looks like three hundred and forty-one dollars and twenty-nine cents."

Wow. That's ridiculous.

"How would you like to pay for that? Cash or credit?"

I turn around and walk away from the counter. Not only is this guy an idiot, but the whole company is run by crooks.

The guy with the clipboard is standing at the door with his hand on it.

"Would you like to fill out our customer satisfaction survey today?"

I look at him. I can't take his goofy smile and empty eyes. I turn around and face the store.

"Screw you all! My dad died and so my cell phone got shut off! Assholes!"

I push by the guy at the door, opening it myself and walk out onto the sidewalk. I take a deep breath and start walking. Not toward Dex's house, but in the way I was already heading.

I'm not going back there without a phone.

After another ten minutes of walking, I come across an independent wireless dealer. I look through the window and see displays for all the major brands, including the place I just came from.

I open the door and go inside. There's one guy working, standing behind a counter, who glances up from a magazine and nods. I would rather ask for help if I need it.

Browsing the displays of the major providers takes only a couple of minutes. I can't really afford any of them, so I'm not sure what I'm going to do.

"Do you have any phones where the plans are a little cheaper?"

"Prepaid phones," he says, without looking up from his magazine.

"Where are those?"

He nods to the left. I walk over to a display for a company I've never heard of before, it must be local, and I start to look at the phones. They're all crappy. Most of them don't even have color screens. I sigh. Am I really going to switch from a Smartphone to one of these? I don't really have much of a choice.

I read over the display to figure out which plan will work. They all have unlimited texting, so it really comes down to the number of minutes and the cost of the plan. I guess I should go with the cheapest one, at least until I have a job and start making some money. I could always bump up to a plan with more minutes.

I pick out the cheapest phone and grab one of the prepaid cards for the cheapest plan. I walk back to the counter and set them down. I see his eyes glance momentarily to my purchase, but he continues to read. He turns the page and finally looks up at me.

"Anything else?"

"That's it."

He scans the phone and the card and then swipes the card to activate it.

"Fifty-four dollars and twenty-two cents."

I set my purse on the counter and count out fifty-five dollars. It's a lot more than I wanted to spend, but I don't see any other option... I need a phone to get a job. I hand over the money and he hands me the card and the phone.

I walk out of the store and turn toward home. I want to get back so I can text Logan with my new number and redo my résumé. It's already late enough in the day that I won't be able to look for a job now... most of the restaurants, which are the most likely to hire me, will be getting ready for dinner service by the time I could get back here.

Ugh. Another wasted day. I've gotta get out of here.

CHAPTER NINE

When I get back to the house I'm starting to feel a little bad about not telling Gina that I was leaving. She might think that Dex is a great guy, but she's been nice to me. I should be nice to her. I can refuse to take a limo, 'cause that's just crazy, but I should at least tell her when I'm leaving the house.

I walk up to the buzzer and press it.

"Yes?"

"Gina, it's me, can you open the gate?"

I can hear her sigh before she lets go of the intercom button. The gate opens and I walk through. Gina is standing at the front door when I walk up, with her arms crossed and an irritated look on her face.

I walk toward her, but she doesn't step aside. She just glares at me and I can see the pure rage in her eyes. I didn't think she actually had it in her.

"What?" I say.

She doesn't say anything. I step forward and she widens her stance to block the door.

"Can I please go inside?"

Gina finally stands to the side and I walk by. I turn toward the stairs, but she grabs my arm. Pain shoots up to my shoulder as her fingernails dig into me.

"I thought we talked about you not leaving by yourself."

I yank my arm free and walk away from her. Is she serious? Who does she think she is? She can't talk to me like that or grab my arm.

"We're not done talking about this," she says, as I run up the stairs and head for my room.

Yes, we are. I'm not going to argue with her and I don't have to do what she tells me. I slam my bedroom door shut, hoping that she hears it.

I sit down on my bed and pull my new phone and the prepaid card out of my purse. I need to text Logan, he always seems to make me feel better no matter what's happening.

I activate the phone and create a new contact for Logan's number.

Hey, it's Amy. My phone got shut off, so this is my new phone number.

I add Jess to my phone while I wait for Logan to text me back.

Hi, I was wondering why you didn't text me back this morning. I miss you.

I feel a little bit better about last night and today when I read his text. It's not quite as good as hearing his voice though.

Do you have time to talk for a few minutes?

When I type on my phone's keypad I can tell how cheaply it's made. Ugh. I can't wait to get a job so I can get a phone that can do more than just text and talk, this is ridiculous.

Actually, I'm about to head to a meeting. Can I text you after?

My heart sinks. I needed to hear his voice and vent a little.

Yeah, that's fine.

Alright, I'll text you later.

I set my phone down on my pillow and walk over to

the window. The lights for the pool turn on even though it's not dark yet. I wish I could go for a swim, it would help me think since I've been missing my morning run. Jess was right, it was good to run in the morning for several reasons. I always got good thinking done and it made me feel less stressed out. I feel so on edge right now.

A swimsuit. Another thing I want to buy, but can't afford. I need to get a job tomorrow, that's all there is to it.

There's a heavy knock on my door. Gina must be mad, but I don't bother turning away from the window. She knocks again, harder this time.

"Mr. Baldwin will be here in ten minutes. You need to be downstairs for dinner."

Great, just what I need. After the last couple of nights I'm starting to think that Dex and my mom are perfect for each other. They're both out of their minds. They deserve each other.

I grab my phone and text Jess while standing at the window.

Hey, it's Amy. My phone got shut off, so this is my new number... for now at least.

My phone chimes as I get a response from her almost instantly.

Hey!! I tried texting you last night and never heard back. I thought maybe you went all Hollywood on me or something.

I can't help but smile. She's ridiculous. I miss her almost as much as I miss Logan.

Never. How are you?

Good. I was thinking about you this morning when I was on my run. What about you? Have you been running?

Now I feel guilty for not running the past few days. I feel like I earned some time off, given everything that's happened.

No, but I was just looking out my window at the pool wishing I could go for a swim.

You should! If I had a pool I would totally swim every day.

I don't have a suit and I can't really afford to buy one since I still don't have a job.

The lights in the pool change color and pull my attention back outside. The last few rays of sunlight are reflecting off the pool. It's beautiful. Not to mention it looks inviting.

And? Do you think me not having a suit would stop me from going swimming?

I laugh. I have a feeling that it wouldn't slow her down one bit and depending on who was here she might even be in the pool faster.

Yeah, but I'm a little more modest than you.

Booo. Just wear underwear then, if you're so worried about someone catching a glimpse.

I don't know why I didn't think of that. I mean, it's not optimal, but it could work until I can afford a suit. If tomorrow is as hot as today was, I might just have to do that.

There's a knock on my door. It's not the angry knock of Gina or her soft touch. It's almost mellow. It can't possibly be my mom, can it? I would think there would be a more aggressive knock if it were her.

"Amy?"

It's Dex.

"Yeah?"

"I brought home a pizza. I would really like it if came down and joined me."

I want to say no, but there's something in his voice... he sounds so sincere. I don't know how to explain it.

"Sure, I'll be right down."

I sigh. Hopefully a dinner of pizza won't last long enough that Dex can be too much of an ass. I grab my phone to text Jess back.

Going to grab dinner, you gonna be around later?

I'm actually just on break at work. I'll text you tomorrow?

Sounds good.

I set my phone down on the nightstand and head downstairs. When I open the door to the kitchen, Dex is sitting at the table with a slice of pizza in his hand. The box is in the middle of the table and there is a plate and a bottle of water in front of my chair. I look around the kitchen for Gina, wondering where she went.

"Gina isn't here, I sent her home."

Weird. I guess I just assumed she was a live-in cook.

"I do let her go home, I'm not *that* mean to her."

He smiles and takes another bite of pizza. No, he's just mean to me. I sit down and reach for a slice. As I pull it free a long string of cheese gets stuck and falls on the table. I glance up at Dex to see if he notices, but he seems lost in his pizza. I scoop the cheese up and put it on the edge of my plate.

I bite into the pizza and burn the crap out of the top of my mouth. I open my mouth and let the pizza fall back to my plate and reach for the bottle of water. It cools it down some, but I can tell at least one layer of skin is gone.

"Are you alright?"

I glare at Dex. Does it look like I'm alright? He looks like he's trying really hard not to laugh.

I take another drink of water and start to stand up from the table. I don't need this. I would rather go hungry than sit across from a man who hates me and finds my misfortune funny. I grab my plate and tuck the bottle of water under my arm.

"Wait... don't leave."

I look Dex in the eyes. I'm so confused when I look at him. The look on his face says he doesn't want me to leave, but his behavior says otherwise. I feel so torn when I'm around him. It's like he's a nice guy who's hiding behind being a Hollywood big shot. It's so strange.

"I'm sorry, but it was kind of funny... you have to admit that."

I turn and walk toward the door. I hear him push his chair away from the table and footsteps coming toward me. I stop when I feel his arm on my shoulder. It's not like when Gina grabbed my arm, it's a softer touch... one that doesn't have anger or irritation behind it. I turn around and look into his eyes.

"Look... I know this situation isn't ideal, but I want to make the best of it, and I want you to know that you're welcome here as long as you want to stay. I really like your mom and I want to get to know you."

Since the moment I stepped through his front door, I just assumed that he wanted me out of here as soon as possible. Maybe I was wrong. I'm getting a totally different vibe from him now.

"Please? Just sit back down so we can talk."

I turn around and look into his eyes. I can tell he's sincere. I nod and he smiles at me. We sit back down at the table.

I blow on my pizza and take a bite. This time it's cool enough to eat and it actually tastes really good. I can't even remember the last time I had a pizza this good. That's one thing I do have to say about here... the food is really good compared to Greenville and Salem. It's a good thing I'm leaving soon.

"What do you think?" Dex says.

"It's really good."

He smiles as I take another bite.

"I'm glad you like it. I probably eat too many of them, usually it's what I eat when Gina has the night off."

We both reach for another slice. Dex lets me grab mine first and then gets his. I smile and take a bite.

"So did you do anything exciting today?"

I guess this is his attempt at getting to know me better. I guess he wants to avoid talking about my past, for good reason. I shrug. There isn't much to say. I'm not going to tell him I sat in bed, feeling depressed all morning before I left to get a phone and pissed off Gina.

"Not really. What about you?"

"It was kind of a boring day, mostly just meetings for the film I start shooting this week."

Without even realizing it, I grabbed a third slice of

pizza while Dex was talking.

"You're doing another movie already?"

He nods as he finishes chewing.

"Yeah, it's a little unusual. Typically, I would finish off the movie I shot earlier this year before starting filming on my next project... but this new one is an indie film with Spencer, so we had to do it when both our schedules allowed."

I'm a little surprised actually. I didn't think a guy like Dex would direct an indie film... I figured he was all about the money.

"You look shocked," he says, with a smile on his face.

"I thought... I don't know... I thought you only made big budget movies."

Dex wipes his hands on a napkin and takes a drink of water.

"I usually do. I like the money, I'm not gonna lie and people seem to like my movies... but sometimes it's nice to do something different."

I finish my third slice and take a drink of water. The pizza was so good, but I'm crazy full now. Dex pushes the box a little closer to me, trying to get me to eat another piece, but I shake my head.

"C'mon, you don't want one more?"

"I'll explode."

He pulls the box toward himself and grabs the last two slices. He looks up and smiles. I smile back. So far this dinner hasn't been the torturesome night I had imagined it to be.

"So... Gina told me that you keep leaving and that you won't let her call a limo for you."

So she did tell him. I figured she wouldn't say anything because she was afraid of getting in trouble.

"Yeah, I can walk, I don't need a limo to drive me around."

Dex just looks at me while he eats. He stares into my eyes and it feels like he can see into my soul and knows my every thought. It's a strange feeling... not bad... just different. I turn away.

"Huh. Most people your age would love to ride in a limo."

I shrug and take a sip of water. Maybe he's finally starting to realize that I'm not like most people my age. I'm trying to get a job... a potential employer would never take me seriously if they saw me pull up in a limo.

"Well... I guess you should get your driver's license then."

That would require me learning to drive and then it still doesn't do much good since I can't afford a car. I mean... I guess I could get my license and then once I move back to Salem I could get a better job and make enough to afford a car. I know Jess could probably get me a job at her work.

"I really don't mind paying for driving lessons for you. I know that trapped feeling you get from not being able to drive around and go where you want."

"Why can't I just walk? I really don't mind."

Dex cringes. It's as if he doesn't want to say and he wishes that I already knew.

"I know you come from a small town. Things here are... different. I don't want you to get in the habit of walking around during the day and creating a false sense of safety for yourself. L.A. is a dangerous place, even Beverly Hills can be dangerous."

He's right. I would have never given a second thought to walking around at night here. I don't know the feeling of being afraid of walking around at night. Greenville was always so safe and Salem didn't seem that much different, even though it's considerably larger.

"Normally I would suggest that Ricardo drive you around, but he went with your mom and her friends to Napa so that he could drive them around while they go wine tasting."

So that's where she is. I can't believe she has already

made good enough friends here that she's rushing off and going wine tasting for days at a time. So crazy. I guess she had no problem going from life as a teacher to being a Hollywood socialite. And apparently the death of my dad had no effect on her.

"I don't want you to have to pay for driving lessons."

Dex frowns and wipes off his mouth with his napkin.

"Why not?"

"That's not your responsibility."

"I know, but I thought it would be nice."

"Thank you, but it's not necessary."

"Let me just do this for you... I really would like that."

I can feel the anger starting to build inside me. Why does he think that he can just throw his money at things and get what he wants?

"No, I'm not comfortable with that."

He bites his lower lip and squints at me. He seems so confused by the fact that his money doesn't tempt me the way it does everyone else. It's like he's never seen it before. I barely keep myself from laughing. I can't believe this guy.

"I'm not trying to replace your dad, don't get that impression, and I'm not trying to get you to like me by using my money. I promise that's not what I want."

I don't even know what to say.

"I know that you want to get out of here and go back to Salem, I get that, and I would have probably wanted the same thing when I was your age... so let me help you. Your mother wants you here until your eighteenth birthday? Fine, let me help make your time here a little easier."

Dex stands up from the table, looks at me and shakes his head and turns toward the door.

"Whatever, you don't want my help. I get it."

Now I feel bad. Maybe there was a part of me that thought he was acting like he was trying to replace my dad and I just didn't want to admit it.

"Wait."

Dex stops, turns around and looks at me. He doesn't look upset or sad... it's like he's disappointed, but I can't tell if it's in me or the fact that I refused his help.

"I'm sorry," I say.

I look into his eyes, those eyes that can see into my soul, and he nods. He knows that I'm sorry and he can tell that even if I'm resistant to his help, it doesn't mean that I don't need or want it... it's just that I'm too afraid to ask for it.

Dex smiles at me briefly, turns and walks out of the kitchen.

CHAPTER TEN

A tiny ray of light is able to squeeze through a hole in my blinds and strikes me right in my left eye. I roll over and pick up my phone to check the time. Ugh... it's just after seven.

Normally I wouldn't care... seven isn't *that* early, but I slept like crap. I kept having weird dreams all night, but now that I'm awake, I can't seem to remember what they were about. I sit up in bed, just glad that the dreams are over, rub the sleep from my eyes and stretch my arms above my head as I yawn.

Another day closer to my birthday and another day closer to leaving this awful place.

I get out of bed and open the blinds. I scan the back yard and notice a man digging and drop to the floor. Hopefully he didn't see me. I scoot along the floor until I'm away from the window and stand up again. I grab some shorts and a shirt and toss them on before heading downstairs.

I hope that Gina has calmed down since yesterday. I know that what I did pissed her off, but she can't just expect me to stay inside the walls like some... some caged animal or princess high in a tower. I have a feeling she thinks of me more as an animal, but I would like to think that I'm more of the princess type. Either way, escape is more pertinent than keeping her happy.

Today is the day that I've gotta find a job. Now that I have a phone again I can actually hand out my résumé, so potential employers can actually contact me.

When I get to the kitchen, Gina isn't around. I pause and listen, but I don't hear anyone. I take a deep breath, assuming that I'm alone in the house and don't have to worry about acting a certain way around anyone else.

I open the fridge and look for something to eat. Nothing really looks that good and I almost close the fridge, but my stomach starts to grumble and I decide I better eat. I grab some yogurt, which is the most fancily packaged yogurt I've ever seen, a bagel and a bottle of water. I open a few drawers until I find a spoon and I sit down at the table in my normal spot.

I pick up the yogurt, realizing I didn't even look to see what flavor it was. It's blueberry and I plunge the spoon into it and stir it so that the fruit is evenly distributed. The smell of fresh blueberries tickles my nose as I lift the first spoonful to my mouth. It tastes amazing! I put the spoon back in the yogurt to get more as a moan escapes my lips.

I don't stop eating the yogurt until I've scraped every last bit from the glass container. I let out a sigh and take a sip of water. I get up from the table, throw the empty yogurt container in the trash and put my spoon in the sink. I grab my water and bagel and head back upstairs. I don't know what the house policy is on eating outside of the kitchen or dining room, but since I'm here alone I'm going to assume it's fine.

I head into the office and power up the computer. I finish half of my bagel before I feel full, not to mention it's not that good untoasted and dry, and I set it down on the edge of the desk.

When the computer starts up, I glance at the two folders off to the side of the desktop that previously caught my attention. I force myself not to think about them and instead just open the word processing program. I open my résumé, glad that I saved it, and change the phone number.

I guess I'm going to need to try a few places, so I print out six copies of the résumé and save the file again before I shut down Dex's computer. I grab the résumés and head out of the room.

I need to shower and get out of here… it's early, but I can stop by that coffee shop now that I have a résumé and go from there. It's going to be a long day, I would have really rather stayed in bed, but I need a job and I need money.

~~~

I grab my phone, put it in my front pocket, and put my purse over my shoulder. I take one last look around my room to make sure I have everything. I grab the résumés off the bookshelf and head out. I step lightly through the house and take the front staircase. I don't want to talk to Gina if I don't have to. I reach for the doorknob and open the door.

I walk toward the front gate and as I do so, a car pulls up and stops at the gate. A man gets out of the car, looks at me and smiles. I have no idea who he is, I've never seen him before.

"Are you Amy?"

Who is this guy? I wrinkle my brow and start walking backward toward the house. I don't want to turn my back to him. I try to memorize his facial features just in case he tries to do something weird and I have to call the cops.

I would guess that he's in his early forties, with short brown hair and a mustache that looks like he's from an 80's cop TV show. He's driving a fairly non-descript car, it's a silver Japanese sedan that I've seen hundreds of times before.

"Amy? I'm Ron, from Ron's driving school. Dex called me and told me that you needed some driving instruction."

What? Is he telling the truth? I freeze and just look at him. He doesn't look like a weirdo or a creeper… but I'm starting to realize that people here in L.A. are not always what they appear.

"Here," he says, walking toward the gate with his hand out, "this is my card."

I take a step forward, but then stop. I remember that the gate opens when a car or person approaches it from this side. If he's not who he says he is, the gate would open and I would lose the only semblance of safety that I have right now.

I feel a shiver pass down my spine… not because I feel unsafe, but because I'm afraid of the unknown. It's a weird feeling. I turn and walk toward the house.

"Wait!"

I don't look over my shoulder. He might not be who he says he is… and I'm not sticking around to find out. If Dex really did call him, which is a possibility since I talked to Dex about driving lessons… I figured Dex would have told me about it before he actually called someone to come teach me to drive.

I go back inside and look out the peephole of the front door. Ron, if that's his name, is holding a phone up to his ear and nodding. I wonder who he could be calling. He nods a few times and puts the phone back in his pocket and walks over to the gate keypad. The gate swings open, he gets back in his car and drives through.

Well… now I feel like a bit of an idiot. He must have called Dex to get the code to the gate since I wouldn't let him in. Now Ron is probably irritated, and so is Dex. Ugh.

He parks his car with the side facing toward the front door and I can clearly see in large lettering down the side it says 'Ron's Driving School' and has his phone number. I kind of feel like an idiot now… for once I wasn't blindly trusting someone and it turns out they were trustworthy. Well, at least in terms of him saying who he was. Ron gets out of his car, walks up to the front door and rings the bell. I stand back, take a deep breath and wait to see if Gina might appear and if I can avoid talking to Ron… but she doesn't.

I pull the door open and try to smile at Ron. I know I made an ass of myself, but I don't want him to know that I'm aware of that. *Just play it cool Amy.*

"Yes?" I say.

"Amy?"

I nod my head. He holds out a business card and I take it from him. It says the same thing as the side of his car, in addition to saying his name 'Ron Oliver' across the middle in red letters. I look up at him and force a smile.

"Sorry… I guess Dex didn't let you know I was coming… so I can understand your reservations to let me through the gate."

"Yeah… he didn't mention you when we talked about the *possibility* of him paying for driving lessons for me."

A wrinkle crosses his brow, but fades in an instant.

"Well… he called me early this morning… I guess on his way to the studio and wanted me to swing by this morning so that we could get you started."

This definitely isn't what I had in mind when I woke up this morning. I still need to text Logan back after last night… I fell asleep as soon as I got in bed. I was going to text him while I was walking… but now I don't know. Do I have to go with Ron? I realize it would be rude at this point, especially with what I just put him through, to ask him to leave, but I just don't know if I can afford to be unemployed for any longer than is absolutely necessary.

On the other hand… it would be really nice to get my driver's license or at least get the ball rolling on it.

"Alright. Just so you know, I've never driven a car before."

Ron cracks a smile at me and nods his head toward the car. He turns and I follow him. He gets in the driver's side and I get in the passenger side. I put on my seatbelt as Ron starts the car and does a three-point turn and waits for the gate to open.

"How come you never drove before?"

He looks both ways and pulls out of the driveway onto the main road.

"I never really needed to… I grew up in a small town and could walk wherever I needed to go."

"Ah, this must be quite a change for you."

"Yeah."

He has no idea. I hold off on telling him that I had always wanted to get my license but my parents insisted that it wasn't necessary and they didn't want me on their car insurance and they both needed their cars. I eventually gave up and knew that I would have to wait until I made enough money to afford all of it on my own.

"How do you like it so far?"

"L.A.?"

"Yeah, do you like living here?"

No. It's awful. Every waking moment I'm pissed at my mom for making me come here. I just want to be back in Salem with Logan.

"I'm looking forward to going home."

"Oh… you don't live here?"

I take a deep breath. I get that Ron's just trying to get to know me a little… I'm sure it's just a part of his job, but it's really starting to irritate me. The more I talk about being here, the more I'm reminded that I'm here against my own will.

"Can we talk about something else?" I say.

Ron glances over at me, but I just keeping looking ahead. We take a few turns and I'm already lost and completely turned around. I can't believe anyone can actually find their way around in a city this size.

"Sure… whatever you want."

"Let's talk about you," I say.

Ron chuckles and cracks a smile.

"Sure," he says. "What would you like to know about me?"

I hadn't really thought it through… I was really just looking for a way to divert the conversation away from me and the fact that I don't want to be here right now.

"How did you become a driving instructor?"

He raises his eyebrow and looks over at me briefly.

"You really want to hear about that? It's not very exciting."

I nod. Anything to change the direction of the conversation.

"Well… I guess I started down this path about twenty years ago when I moved here from Iowa. I had this grand vision of becoming the next big actor. It turned out that I was crap at acting but I could drive well."

Ron pauses as he takes a right turn and merges onto a four lane freeway. The traffic is awful, worse than anything I've ever seen, but it doesn't seem to faze him.

"And so I started working as a professional driver for movies, at first doing simple stuff like driving cars that were in the background of shots or passing by. I practiced driving maneuvers in empty parking lots on my days off and eventually I got offered a gig doing chase scene driving, and that kind of stuff, for one of the big production companies."

We take an exit and turn down one of the side streets. The small homes are soon replaced by industrial looking buildings, most of which look run down and abandoned.

"Should I keep going? I did warn you that the story was boring…."

"No, it's interesting."

It's true. I find it fascinating that someone could move here with grand dreams and when they don't work out still make a life for themselves. It's amazing.

"Well… it got to be a dangerous and hard way to make

a living and as I got older I realized I wanted a job where I wasn't constantly risking my life so I founded Ron's Driving School."

"So you teach driving to young people now? That's so different from being a driver for movies."

Ron chuckles as he turns into the driveway of an industrial complex and brings the car to a stop in front of a gate. He rolls his window down, reaches out and punches a code into the keypad. The gate buzzes and slowly opens.

"Not really... I teach people how to be stunt drivers for movies and I also have some guys who work for me that I lease out to studios. That's how I met Dexter, he uses a couple of my guys in almost all of his movies."

That made sense. It seems like everyone here has some relation to the movie industry.

"I'm just doing this as a favor to Dex... I owe him much of my success and he always calls me first when he needs drivers for his movies."

Huh. Another person, just like Gina, who thinks Dex is some sort of great guy. I'm the only one who doesn't see it or did he pull the wool over their eyes?

Ron pulls the car through the now open gate. It closes behind us and Ron drives the car between two clearly abandoned warehouses. Just beyond them is a large paved area the size of a parking lot at a large chain grocery store. The surface is worn with visible cracks across it and weeds sprouting up everywhere.

This place is a little odd... and definitely not a place I would ever want to be alone. It looks almost like it could be the set of a horror film. Heck... it probably was at some point.

"What... what is this place?"

Ron laughs. I think he can sense the hesitation in my voice.

"This is my training grounds. The warehouses have handling courses set up inside and this open area is used to learn other maneuvers. I figured since you're technically not allowed on the streets I would bring you here and teach you."

Ron stops the car, turns to me and smiles. I smile back at him, he seems like a genuinely nice guy and I feel bad for doubting who he was back at the house.

"Alright, let's get started."

We both get out of the car and switch spots. I buckle my seatbelt, wrap my fingers around the wheel and take a deep breath.

"It's fine… it's an open lot… you won't hit anything and once you get the hang of it you're going to love the freedom that comes with being able to drive a car."

I nod my head. I know he's right, but right now my heart feels like it's about to beat out of my chest. *You can do this, Amy, it's not a big deal… millions of people drive every day.*

"Alright, now put your foot on the brake, the left pedal, and shift the car into drive."

I nod, take another deep breath, and do what Ron says.

"OK, now what?"

"Now slowly let your foot off the brake. Don't press the gas yet."

I lessen the pressure I'm applying on the brake and the car starts to roll forward.

"Aaah!"

I mash my foot back down on the brake and the car stops. I'm shaking so bad that I can't even look over at Ron when he starts laughing. I finally turn my head and glare at him, once I've calmed down some, but he keeps laughing.

"It's not funny!"

He forces himself to stop and clears his throat.

"Sorry, you're right, it's not funny."

I can't tell if he's being serious or not. I get my answer when his serious look dissolves and is replaced by an infectious smile. Before I know it we're both laughing at the absurdity of the situation.

"See, it's funny," he says.

I shake my head. He's right, I overreacted to a completely normal part of driving. We both finally settle back down and I grip the steering wheel again and look over at Ron.

"OK, let's try that again. Just remember, this is a huge open lot, so you're not going to crash into anything unless you smash the gas pedal down and don't take your foot off. Just let your foot off the brake and drive around."

I nod and follow his directions. This time when the car rolls forward I don't freak out, but I keep my foot hovering right over the brake as if a kid or a dog might run in front of the car at any moment.

"Try to relax, it will make it easier," Ron says.

I relax my grip on the steering wheel and sit back in my seat. He's right, there's not really anything to be afraid of, not in this lot at least.

"Good, good. Now turn to the left and drive to the other side of the lot without using the gas."

I glance down at the speedometer, which is barely registering any speed even though I feel like we're moving around the lot at breakneck speeds. It's a crazy sensation. Driving a car is nothing like riding in the passenger seat.

"So do you have any friends here?"

"No, I just moved here from Salem."

I have a feeling that Ron isn't really interested in my life story, but is really just trying to get me to relax and it seems to be working. Before I know it, I'm feeling more confident and my foot is hovering over the gas pedal instead of the brake… just waiting for him to tell me I'm ready.

"If you want, I can give you my daughter's phone number… she's about your age and she can take you around town and show you the places that girls your age go."

Usually I would say no, there's really no reason for me to make friends since I'm leaving here so soon, but Ron seems super cool and I don't see the harm in making one friend. Heck, it might even make the time between now and my birthday go a little quicker.

"You don't think she would mind?"

"Nah, she's just mostly hanging out at home, waiting for school to start again."

"Alright, I guess that would be cool."

Maybe my time here isn't going to feel like it's dragging on forever. Now I just need to find a job and I'll be set.

CHAPTER ELEVEN

"Thanks again, Ron, I really appreciate it."

He smiles at me and waves from the car.

"No problem, Amy. Just give me a call later this week and we can set up another lesson. And give Jen a call, I'm sure she'd like to hang out with you this week."

"I will."

I turn and walk to the front door and push it open. I close the door and head toward the kitchen. I can feel my body finally starting to come down from the rush of driving and I'm starting to feel hungry. I guess it's possible that driving, and the level of focus it requires, used a lot more energy than I realized.

I freeze when I walk into the kitchen and see Gina. She's standing at the sink with her back to me. Maybe if I'm quiet I can leave and she won't notice. I turn and in the process bump into the wall. I freeze, but it's too late. Gina turns around and sees me.

"Hi," she says, smiling at me.

I wonder why she's in such a good mood.

"Hi."

"Did you want me to make you something to eat?"

"It's alright," I say. "I'm sure I can find something in

the fridge."

As I walk toward the fridge, Gina turns off the sink and dries her hands and gets to the fridge before I can.

"Sit, I'll make you something."

"Thanks."

I sit down at my normal spot and pull out my phone. I still haven't had a chance to text Logan and I'm starting to really miss talking to him. When I check my phone, there isn't a message from him and my heart sinks. There's not even a message from Jess. So strange. I write a message to Logan and hit send.

Sorry, I fell asleep last night as soon as I got in bed. How are you? I miss you. How is practice?

I decide to hold off on texting Jess for now. I *do* want to talk to her, but if Logan responds I want to focus on talking to him. Gina walks over to me and sets down a plate and a bottle of water.

"Thanks."

Gina walks away and I look down at the plate. On it is a peanut butter and jelly sandwich, made with the same delicious bread she used for grilled cheese with the other day, and some potato chips. I pop one of the chips in my mouth and chew it while I open the bottle of water.

I keep meaning to ask why we always drink bottled water... I mean, I figure it has something to do with the quality of the water here, but I'm not sure. Maybe I don't want to know... I still have to shower and brush my teeth with the tap water.

I pick up half of the sandwich and take a bite. Crunchy peanut butter and blueberry jelly ooze into my mouth. It tastes amazing. It's not like any other PB&J I've ever had... I mean it's all the same things in it... but this one just tastes so much better.

"How's your sandwich?"

I turn to Gina and quickly finish chewing.

"It's really good, thank you."

She smiles and turns back to the stove. I take another

bite of my sandwich and watch as she scrubs the stove-top. I wonder how she can possibly be so happy most of the time being a cook and having to clean up. She can't possibly make very much money. She turns around and I quickly turn my head with the hope that she didn't notice my watching her.

I put the last bite of PB&J into my mouth as my phone vibrates. I wipe my hands on my napkin and pick it up. My stomach feels like it's full of butterflies as I read the text from Logan.

Hey, beautiful. I figured as much. I'm good, just got home from my morning practice. How's the job search going?

Ugh… the job search. I know that I probably shouldn't have blown off the job search to go driving, but I'm still glad that I did. Ron was right, driving instantly gave me a feeling of independence that I never knew I was missing and now I couldn't wait to get behind the wheel of a car again.

I'm just having some lunch right now and then I'm going out to look. I was doing a driving lesson this morning.

I eat the last of my chips and take another drink of water. Before I can stand up to put my plate in the dishwasher, Gina is already standing at the table and picks up the plate. She smiles at me and I smile back. I guess she's not mad at me anymore.

"Thanks."

"You're welcome."

My phone vibrates and I look down to read the text from Logan.

Oooh, fancy. Driving lessons. How was it?

It was fun, I liked it. I'm going again next week. The guy, Ron, is a former driver for movies and he's a really nice guy.

I stand up from the table and turn toward Gina. She's at the sink, washing dishes again. I bite my lip and try to decide if I should tell her I'm leaving. I know she keeps getting upset about me walking, but I'm *not* taking a limo. Before I can decide she turns around and looks right at me. I feel like she's reading me like a book and can tell exactly what I'm thinking.

"If you want to go out, and you won't take a limo, will you let me drive you?" she says.

It's a little scary that she was able to just look at me and know that I wanted to leave, but I was waiting to see what her reaction would be.

"I don't want to take away from your work."

"It's fine, I'm caught up. Let me just get my purse. I'll meet you outside."

I head outside to wait for Gina. My phone vibrates and I read the text from Logan.

Awesome, maybe you can drive me around when you get back here.

I laugh. Logan is the only person I've ever known that can be funny over text messages. It seems like usually humor is lost because of the lack of personal delivery, but he somehow manages to be funny without sounding stupid.

Yeah, you just have to let me drive your SUV.

We'll talk again when you actually get your license and you've been driving for more than a few hours.

Gina comes outside and closes the door. We walk over to her car and I'm a little surprised that she can afford something this nice on whatever it is that she makes. I text Logan while we wait for the gate to open.

I'm heading to look for a job right now. Can I text you later?

Yeah, I'll be around after nine.

I put my phone in my purse and pull out a copy of my résumé to read over. I want to make sure that everything is right and that I have most of it memorized, just in case they ask me any questions.

"What's that?" Gina says.

I look up and she points at the résumé.

"My résumé, that's why I keep leaving... I'm trying to find a job."

She wrinkles her brow and stares at me for a moment

before turning her attention back to the gate which is now open. She drives through and turns onto the main road.

"How come?"

"Why am I trying to get a job?"

"Yeah, you don't need the money… why don't you just find a hobby or something to occupy your time?"

I don't need the money? Does she think I'm rich or something?

"I need money so that I can move back to Salem after my birthday."

Gina is silent, perhaps she's realized that she doesn't know all that much about me or why I'm really here. I don't really feel like explaining it to her, not to mention it's not really any of her business.

When we reach Santa Monica Boulevard she turns to me.

"Where am I taking you?"

"Turn left."

When I see the corner where the coffee shop is, I point at it.

"There."

Gina looks for a parking spot and finds one less than a block away.

"I'll be here waiting for you."

I grab my purse, get out of the car and walk back up the street to the closest intersection. If I were in Greenville, or even in Salem, I would just cross… but there's way too much traffic here for that. I wait for the light to change before I walk.

As I walk toward the coffee shop I get a copy of my résumé out and take a deep breath. *You can do this, Amy, you are just as good as any of the people working here… and you aren't a jerk like pretty much everyone in this town.* They have no reason not to hire me. I pull the door handle and walk inside.

There's a bit of a line, which is surprising since it's sometime around one, so I wait until I reach the counter. It's the same girl that was irritated by my presence the other day, but I can tell by the look on her face that she doesn't recognize me.

"What can I get started for you?"

"Oh, um… can I talk to Ted?"

I look behind the counter to see if he's around, but I don't see him.

She rolls her eyes at me and puts her hand on her hip.

"He's not here."

I bite my lip and wonder why she's suddenly gone from the chipper girl to the bitch who wants nothing to do with me since I'm not buying anything. I extend my résumé to her, but she just stands there staring at me.

"Can you give this to him for me, please?"

She rolls her eyes again and lets out an exaggerated sigh, but she takes it from me and puts it under the counter.

"Next," she says, looking by me as if I wasn't still standing in front of her.

I move to the side so that the person in line behind me can step forward, but I continue to glare at the rude girl behind the counter. It's one of those times in life where I wish I could scream and tell her off… but I need a job more than I need to feel better about her being rude.

I shake my head, still amazed at how people act here, and walk out of the coffee shop. I was really hoping that I would have a good shot at getting a job at the coffee shop because after my last two jobs, both at restaurants, I feel like I want to do something different. I don't see many options at this point though….

I do something I wanted to avoid and I walk down the street toward the clothing store where the girls laughed at me. I hope that they aren't working today… I'm not sure that I can take that a second time.

I walk down the street toward the clothing store and try to clear my mind. There's no sense in getting worked up over something that might not even happen. I pull out another copy of my résumé as I get close and take a deep breath as I reach for the door handle. *You can do this, Amy, don't be afraid.*

I put a smile on my face and walk inside. As soon as I look at the counter near the back of the store I can see that it's the same two girls working. I want to turn around and walk out of the store, I really do, but I know I can't.

I walk up to the counter and before I can say anything they look at each other and start giggling. Clearly, unlike the girl in the coffee shop, they recognize me. Great. I shouldn't care, it's not like they're in charge, they must have a manager or something I can talk to.

"Is the manager here?"

They look at each other and then back at me. It's obvious they are trying not to laugh in my face.

"Is the manager here?" I ask again, my voice harder this time.

The girl on the left shakes her head and looks down. She looks a little unnerved by the tone of my voice. I turn to the girl on the right and glare at her. She doesn't flinch, her eyes locked on mine.

"No," she says.

I slap my résumé on the counter and push it toward her.

"Make sure he or she gets this."

She looks down at the paper, but doesn't pick it up. I turn and walk out of the store, knowing full well that they are going to laugh at me once I'm outside. I have a feeling they're probably never going to give my résumé to their manager. At least I tried… and I guess there's always a remote possibility the manager sees my résumé.

I walk back to the car, slightly irritated that I really didn't make any headway for how late in the day it is. I feel like every day when I wake up that I'm just going to be able to walk down the street and get a job, like I did in Greenville and in Salem. I guess maybe things here aren't as easy.

I get back in the car, buckle my seat belt and pull out

my phone. I know Logan is probably busy, but I was hoping that maybe he still sent me a text. There's nothing from him and put my phone back in my purse as Gina pulls out of the parking spot.

"Where to now?"

"I don't know… I only had two places where I wanted to apply and figured if I saw another place I would apply there, too."

I admit, it wasn't the most well thought out plan. I just didn't think that Gina would be driving me around… I thought I would be able to scope out the area and try to find something. Now I feel bad about her having to do this.

"Well… I could drive you around some and just look for places that might look good."

I shake my head. I don't want her to waste the rest of her day driving me around, that would be stupid.

"Let's just go back," I say.

"You sure?"

I nod. I'm not sure what I'm going to do.

"You should look on the Internet," Gina says.

I hadn't thought of that and I'm not sure why. I guess in Greenville when I needed a job there wasn't exactly a lot of places in town, so when one of them was hiring everyone knew about it. In Salem I didn't have a computer and it was easy to find a job there.

"Yeah, maybe I'll do that."

I would rather not, but I know it's the easiest thing to do. Walking the nearby streets while looking for a job would be a much easier way to learn the area. I just know that I'm going to keep upsetting Gina if I constantly sneak out.

However I do it, I need to find a job and quickly. My birthday is getting closer and so far I've only spent money since I got here.

CHAPTER TWELVE

I stand up from my bed, look down at my phone and walk over to the window. I want to text Logan and tell him what happened today, but I know he's busy with football. I need to stop relying on him to listen to me when I'm feeling down, it's not right, he doesn't need or deserve that.

I look at the pool and think that maybe I need to get some exercise. Maybe that will bring me out of this funk I'm in and motivate me to look for a job, because right now it's at a standstill. I can't ask Gina to drive me around again, so I'm going to have to start looking online and I'm putting that off... and I'm not really even sure why.

My last conversation with Jess pops into my head and I realize she's right, I could just wear my bra and panties to swim in, it's not that big of a deal. It's still midafternoon so the only person that might see me is Gina, which I'm not too worried about. I wouldn't want Dex to see me like that, but if the last few days are any indication, he probably won't be home for a few hours at least.

I grab a towel out of my bathroom and strip down to my bra and panties. I wrap the towel around myself and head downstairs. I know Dex said there were towels for the pool in the supply closet, but I don't feel like walking through the house in my underwear. I hear the water in the kitchen running, so I stick my head through the doorway.

"I'm going for a swim."

Gina turns around from the sink and smiles. The look on her face says that she wants to know why I felt the need to inform her of that. I turn around and walk toward the door that leads to the porch and I head outside. A light breeze washes over my face as I walk toward the pool.

I look around as I drop my towel on one of the chairs next to the pool. If the people back home could see me now… I'm sure they wouldn't believe it even if they saw it with their own eyes.

I dip my toe into the pool and yank it out. The pool is frigid. I almost want to skip going in, but I know I need the exercise and it will help me clear my mind. I guess it's better to get it over with quickly. I close my eyes and dive into the pool. The shock of the cold water makes me instantly regret that decision.

It takes a few laps for me to get warmed up, but I'm feeling better and my body feels good. I wish I would have done this sooner. It's relaxing and at the same time it's a good workout, but it doesn't require me to wake up so freaking early like running with Jess did.

On my ninth lap, not that I was counting or anything, I see a figure walking from the house toward the pool. I put my head down, finish the lap and put my arms over the end of the pool as I lift my head out of the water.

I assumed it would Gina, or maybe Dex or maybe even my mom, but standing three feet in front of me is Spencer. He cracks a huge smile at me, walks over to one of the chairs and sits down.

"How are you?"

I'm so surprised to see him that I don't even know what to say. I was really enjoying my swim and wasn't quite ready to stop, but I can't exactly ignore him and keep going.

"I'm fine."

He nods and scoots the chair a little closer to the pool. I feel my arms slipping on the wet concrete, so I pull myself back up. Spencer raises his eyebrow as he watches me and I can tell that I lifted myself a little too high and he was able to see my bra. I feel my face turning red. Great.

I want to lower myself back into the water and just wait for him to leave, but that would be rude and I have a feeling that he might just sit there. I have no idea why he's even here.

"So, did you hear back from Logan about signing an autograph for me?"

Crap. I had texted Logan that night when Spencer asked, but I hadn't talked to him about it since then.

"Sorry, I didn't bring it up with him again. I'll ask him tonight."

"Thanks."

"Did you come all the way here just for that?"

My teeth start chattering. I'm freezing, just sitting in the water. I need to get out or start swimming again.

"No, I came to see Dex."

"He's not here."

"Yeah, that's what Gina said, but she said you were back here so I thought I would pop out to say hi and see how you're doing."

Weird. Why would he even care? We met once and he's a Hollywood heartthrob and I'm... nothing special, I'm just me.

"What?" he says.

"I didn't say anything."

"No, but you had a crazy look on your face, like you were confused and irritated."

I had no idea I was being that transparent.

"Oh, sorry... it's nothing."

Spencer shrugs and cracks a huge white smile. I'm starting to see why all my friends in high school had his picture in their locker... he really is nice to look at. I feel my face turning red again and I push my thoughts about him out of my mind.

"Are you cold?"

I shake my head. I don't want to get out of the pool, not while Spencer is standing there.

"Cause you look like you're freezing."

He's right, I am. I let go of the side of the pool and swim to the shallow end, where I can stand up, and I wrap my arms around my body to try and keep myself warm. Spencer gets up and walks to where I'm standing. He walks to the edge of the pool and extends his arm toward me.

"You've gotta get out of the pool, you look cold."

I know he's right, I was just hoping that he wouldn't see me almost naked.

I hold my hand out and he wraps his hand around my wrist and in one fluid motion pulls me out of the pool. The instant he lets go of me I rush over to the chair and get my towel and wrap it around myself. I hope that he didn't see too much.

I turn back to Spencer, who is still standing at the side of the pool with a huge grin on his face.

"What?"

I think he can sense my irritation. His smile slowly fades, so I don't think so… either that or he really doesn't care.

"Oh, nothing…."

I roll my eyes at him and he just keeps smiling. I walk by him and inside, leaving the door open. I hear him close it as I head toward the stairs. I'm so embarrassed, and irritated by that smug look on his face, that I run up the stairs to my room. I know it's the only place he won't follow me. At least I hope that he won't.

Once I'm in my room, I close my door and put my ear against it. I take a deep breath after a minute when I don't hear anything and I go into the bathroom. I need to get out of my wet underwear as soon as possible.

I hang the towel over the rack and I catch a glimpse of myself in the mirror. I turn toward it and my jaw almost drops. No wonder Spencer was looking at me funny. My wet bra is completely see-through. I'm mortified. I walk out of the bathroom, unable to even look at myself because I can't stop thinking about what he saw, and I quickly change into a T-shirt and some sweats.

I dive under the covers of my bed and pull them over my head. I don't want to ever show my face again, especially if Spencer is around and I have no idea if he's still here.

My phone, which I left sitting on my nightstand while I went for a swim, chirps to let me know I have a text waiting for me. I reach my arm out from under the covers and grab it. Anticipating a text from Logan, and thinking if I should tell him what just happened with Spencer, I feel relieved when I see the message is from Jess.

Hey, just checking in to see how it's going. Been hanging out with any movie stars lately?

I don't know if I should tell her what just happened with Spencer... I mean, she's the only one I could tell, but I'm not sure if it's a good idea.

Can you keep a secret?

Ugh. I instantly know that I shouldn't have said anything to her, and if I had thought longer about it I probably wouldn't have. Too late now, I guess.

Yeah, what happened? Is everything OK?

Everything is fine... I followed your advice and now I think Spencer has a fairly good idea of what I look like naked.

What?!? I never told you to show yourself off to him!

I laugh. She's ridiculous and she's right... she never said that.

No, but you told me to go for a swim wearing my underwear. So I did just that and then he showed up randomly and stood there, talking to me until I got out of the pool. I was embarrassed and ran inside and then I noticed that my bra was see-through.

Repeating it to Jess makes me more aware of how

absurd the whole thing is. I'm not sure that I'll ever be able to face Spencer again. Maybe when I hear back from Logan about the autograph, I can give it to Dex and he can give it to Spencer. That would be best.

OMG! That's freaking hilarious.

I'm glad she finds it funny, because I don't want to ever set foot in public again for fear that I might run into Spencer. I know it's not possible, or even practical, since there's always a chance he could show up wherever I get a job, but I would if I could.

How is that funny? I'm so sure that Spencer Thomas, Hollywood actor and heartthrob, saw me almost naked. I hope I never see him again.

Why would you hope that? I bet he liked what he saw.

I doubted that. The smile on his face suggested that he was amused by what he saw. It kind of reminded me a little of the look on Logan's face the first time I met him.

Not likely.

Why not? You're pretty and he's a good looking guy. I see nothing wrong with that scenario.

The thought hadn't even crossed my mind. Not only would a guy like Spencer ever look at me *that* way, but I have Logan and I don't want to even think about jeopardizing that.

Because... I have Logan, so I don't want to even think about Spencer in that way. As far as I'm concerned, he's just another guy.

I wish I would have never gone for that swim, it's going to be the death of me. So much for trying to get some exercise and get a grip on what I'm going to do about getting a job. Now all I can think about is Spencer, Logan and the little show I just put on. Ugh.

He's not just some guy, Amy, he's Spencer Thomas....

I don't know what's gotten into Jess, but it's kind of starting to irritate me. She's acting like he's some... I don't know, like he's the most important person in the world. I get that he's famous, but that doesn't really matter.

He is just a guy... plus I'm with Logan.

I hope that Jess doesn't tell Logan about this, I doubt she would since I asked her if she could keep a secret....

All I'm saying is that if I was you, I would be embracing the interest that Spencer is showing in you, that's all.

Seriously? What doesn't she get about my relationship with Logan? I really want to text her back and tell her how mad I am, but I don't think there's even a point.

I close my eyes and take a deep breath. Why do things have to be so complicated? I just want life to be easy.

~~~

A knock on my door wakes me. I look at my phone, it's just after six o'clock. I must have fallen asleep after texting Jess without even really trying. A second knock prompts me to get out of bed and walk to the door. I stretch my arms as I walk, which feel kind of sore... which I guess is the result of swimming. I'm going to have to keep at it, but I definitely need to buy a bathing suit first.

I open the door and I'm greeted by Dex, who has a huge smile on his face.

"You ready for dinner?"

"I guess?"

"You don't sound so sure..."

I blink my eyes a few times to try and wake myself up.

"No, I just woke up."

Dex laughs and shakes his head.

"Alright, well when you're awake, why don't you come downstairs and have dinner with me."

"Sure."

He turns and walks toward the stairs.

"Oh and I have a surprise for you," he says, disappearing downstairs before I can respond.

What does that mean? A surprise? I close the door and sit down on my bed. A thousand thoughts rush through

my head, most of them not good. It could be anything…
maybe my mom is back or maybe Spencer is over for
dinner again…. Those two stick out as the worst. I really
hope it's not either of them.

I close my eyes, take two deep breaths and try to calm
myself down. I know that I'm going to have to talk to my
mom at some point, that's inevitable, so there's not much I
can do about that. If it's Spencer… well… I'm not sure
what I'm going to do, I just hope that he doesn't mention
this afternoon to Dex. That would be more than I could
take.

I head downstairs and it's just Dex sitting at the table.

"Are you alright?"

I pull out my chair and sit down.

"Yeah, why?"

"Oh, you just had a look on your face."

Apparently I'm terrible at hiding my emotions. I flash a
smile at Dex and open my bottle of water.

"No, everything is good."

I drink some water so that I don't have to say anything
else, although I'm really relieved that my mom or Spencer
isn't here. I'm starting to not mind having dinner with Dex
as much and the food is always good.

Dex smiles at me and pushes a small brown box across
the table. I must have been too preoccupied to notice it
when I first sat down.

"What is it?"

"It would spoil the surprise if I told you what it is."

I reach and grab the box. It feels fairly light, maybe a
pound or less. I wonder what the heck it could be. The last
thing I wanted was to feel like I owe Dex something, but
after the driving lesson this morning and whatever is in the
box….

I rip open the box and inside is a new Smartphone. It's
the same brand as my old one, but a newer model.

"I didn't know this model was out yet."

"It's not for another month."

I look up and Dex winks at me.

"How…?"

He shrugs, takes a drink of his water and leans back as Gina sets a plate down in front of him.

"I'm friends with the CEO and he hooks me up whenever a new model comes out."

Wow. I'm not even sure what to say. Part of me thinks that Dex is just giving me this to try and ease his guilt for breaking up my family, but when I look into his eyes it seems like he's doing it because he cares about me. It's strange, I'm not sure what to do.

"I already have a phone."

Dex shrugs as he picks up his fork, spears a piece of broccoli and puts it in his mouth. I lift a forkful of salad to my mouth and chew the leafy greens.

"Well, you don't have to use it if you don't want… but you said your phone had been shut off and I know that teenage girls can't live without a cell phone."

He takes a drink of water before he continues.

"If you don't want it, I'll take it back."

Now I just feel like an ass. I didn't mention to him that I went out and bought my cheap prepaid phone the other day, so it seems like in this case he did actually have no motivation behind giving me the phone. Even though he seems genuine, I can't forget that he broke up my family.

"Thank you."

He smiles at me. I know that I should say something more, but I can't… and when I look into his eyes I can tell that he understands.

~~~

When I get to my room after dinner, I turn on my new phone and set it up. I transfer the few numbers I still care about and then text Logan.

Hey, it's Amy, I got a new phone today and this is my new number. Hope you're having a wonderful day.

I think about texting Jess to tell her about my new number... but I hesitate because of our earlier conversation. It was just so weird.

I'm still finding it strange that Dex is being seemingly super nice the last couple days and I'm starting to wonder what his motivation could possibly be. It could be that he's trying to bond with me before my mom gets back to show how good of a guy he is or he could be feeling guilty for the destruction of my family. Either way I want to find out. Not that it really matters, but I think it might make me feel better.

I miss Logan. Not being able to see him is already harder than I thought it would be. I don't know how the heck I'm going to make it until my birthday. My new phone chirps and I smile when I see the text from Logan.

Hey, beautiful, it's nice to hear from you. Look at you, all fancy with another new phone.

I laugh. Yeah, fancy, that's me.

It was a gift from Dex, so whatever, but at least I don't have to keep using that crappy prepaid phone. I wish I hadn't spent the money on it.

I guess I can just keep if for emergencies, it's not like the worst thing to ever happen.

Oh, nice. Well, now at least you don't have to worry about paying for a phone or running out of minutes and texts.

Yeah, you're right. So, how was your day?

It was alright, I was on the field for the first time today doing non-contact drills. It was strange to be out there again, but it was good. My knee isn't quite there yet, so I have to be careful, I don't want to injure it again.

That makes sense. Well, I hope it keeps getting better.

I know how much football means to Logan, I can see the same look in his eyes that I used to see in Mitch's. An intense look that I've never seen in anyone else's eyes.

Thanks. I'm pretty sure that I'll be ready for the start of the season.

Good.

That reminds me, you wanted an autograph for someone? I signed one of the publicity photos from last year and I can send it wherever you want.

I don't know where Spencer lives, so I text Logan the address for Dex's house.

Alright, I'll mail it out tomorrow. Just make sure you open it first, I'm sending you a little something.

My face lights up with a smile, he's so sweet. I can't wait to see what he's sending me.

You're so cute.

I hope that my dreams tonight are filled with my quarterback.

CHAPTER THIRTEEN

Gina is in the kitchen cleaning by the time I get down there. She turns around and smiles at me as I make my way to the fridge to grab a bottle of water.

"You hungry?"

I shrug, I'm kind of hungry… but I haven't been working out, other than my one short swim yesterday, and I feel like I'm eating too much of Gina's cooking. I have a feeling if I'm not careful it's going to start showing when I step on the scale.

"Why don't you sit down and I'll make you a light breakfast. I can always make you something to eat later if you get hungry."

I smile at Gina and walk over to the table and sit down. It's a weird feeling having someone cook for you pretty much every meal, not that I'm complaining, and I think I'm going to miss it once I leave.

I feel my phone vibrate and hoping that it's Logan, I pull it out of my pocket. I wrinkle my nose at the text.

Hey, Amy, I forgot to bring one of the script re-writes for today's shoot. I'm sending a car to the house. I need you to grab it out of my office, it's right on the desk and it's labeled 'Project AC', and bring it down here for me. The car should be there in twenty minutes to pick you up. Thanks. Dex.

Seriously? I guess I should have expected this since he gave me a phone. Well, I guess between the food and the phone and the fact that I'm staying here, I can't complain too much about having to bring him something. The worst part is that I was planning to look for jobs all day.

I jump up from the table and turn to Gina as I walk out of the kitchen.

"Dex is sending a car for me, I've gotta shower."

I head upstairs and hop in the shower. Hopefully it won't take too long to deliver his script. I've gotta find a job today or at least a couple of good leads. I can't keep putting it off or I'm going to be stuck here after my birthday and have no way to get back to Salem in time for the start to school.

I dry myself off and check my phone to see how much time I have left. Crap, the car is going to be here in five minutes and I still have to get dressed and get downstairs. I pull on a pair of jeans, a black shirt and grab my purse and phone.

I find the file easily enough, it was sitting on top of the keyboard, and head downstairs just as the doorbell rings. I walk toward the door as Gina walks out of the kitchen and toward me with a brown paper bag.

"Here, you need to eat something."

"Thanks," I say, smiling at her as I turn the doorknob.

When I get outside there's a large black sedan, with tinted windows, waiting in the driveway. A man in a black suit and dark sunglasses gets out of the driver's side and walks around to the back door, on the passenger's side, and holds it open for me.

"Thanks," I say, as I get in the car.

He closes the door without saying anything and gets back in the driver's seat. We wait for the gate to open and he pulls the car onto the main road.

I pull out my phone and check to see if Logan has texted me yet. When we talked last night he said he would text me this morning before practice, but so far nothing.

After five minutes I'm lost and have no concept of where we are and nothing looks familiar.

"Where are we going?"

"The studio."

OK… well that was helpful. I'm not going to waste my breath on talking to him.

After fifteen minutes of driving downside roads we pull up to the gate of an unassuming compound, which I guess must be where the studio is. The driver stops the car at a security checkpoint, a guard raises the barrier and waves us through.

He pulls up to one of the non-descript warehouse buildings, stops the car and gets out to open my door. I get out, checking to make sure I have all of my things and look around for Dex. There are dozens of people rushing around, but I don't see Dex anywhere.

"Where's…."

He cuts me off and points toward the large door of the closest building. Alright, thanks so much for your help. He's just another person that confirms my suspicion that everyone here is an ass.

Inside the building looks even bigger than from the outside. The whole thing is full of equipment and movie sets. It's kind of surreal to be standing here. For a small town girl like me, it's crazy that I'm standing in a Hollywood studio and I'm bringing a package to the director who has my cell phone number. It feels a little dreamlike actually, and I don't think I'll ever forget this moment.

"Hey! Who are you?"

I turn and see a man with a clipboard pointing his index finger in my face.

"Where's your badge? You're not one of the actors, I know all of them."

"Uh… I'm Amy."

He quickly scans the top sheet of paper on his

clipboard while shaking his head.

"You're not on the list. I'm calling security."

He turns and walks toward the door.

"Wait!" I say, but he doesn't seem to care.

I feel a tap on my shoulder and turn around. Spencer is standing inches away from me with a huge smile on his face. I can tell he's been watching and is quite amused by what just happened.

"What did you do now?"

I can feel my face turning bright red, but I can't tell if it's from embarrassment because of what happened last time I saw Spencer or if it's because I'm mad at him for standing there while the clipboard guy grilled me and he didn't try to rescue me. He could have easily gotten the guys attention and told him who I was.

"That's her!"

We both turn to the clipboard guy as he rushes toward me with two burly security guards in tow.

I feel like I'm in a movie, which I guess given where I am is a little ironic.

Spencer holds up his hands and clipboard guy and the guards slow. They walk up to us, still looking like all three of them are ready to tackle me at a moment's notice.

"It's fine, she's with me."

I want to speak up and explain that I'm in fact not with him, and that I'm actually here to bring Dex a script, but I don't want to open my mouth. I don't think they'll believe me anyway.

The clipboard guy glares at me one last time before turning around and leaving with his burly henchmen in tow.

Spencer puts his hand on my shoulder and starts laughing. I grind my teeth and shrug my shoulder so that his hand falls. He doesn't seem to care and just keeps laughing.

I start to walk away, not really knowing where I'm going, and Spencer catches up with me.

"So, why are you really here? I would like to believe that it's to see me, but I have a feeling that's not the case."

I really want to smack him, I do, but I hold off. Would it be possible for his ego to be any bigger?

"I'm here to deliver this," I say, holding up the folder, "to Dex. Do you know where he is?"

He smiles at me and nods.

"Yeah, come with me."

I follow him to the back of the building through a maze of people and equipment to a set, made to look like a modern bathroom. Dex is talking to a woman, but stops when he sees us. He smiles at us, utters something to the woman and walks over.

"Amy, Spencer, how are you?"

I hand him the folder and he smiles.

"Thank you, so much, you're a life saver. I hope my text didn't wake you up this morning."

"Nope."

Dex turns his head to the right and looks around.

"Where the heck is she…?"

"Who?" Spencer says.

"My assistant. I swear, every time I turn my back, she just vanishes. It's starting to get old."

Out of the corner of my eye I see Spencer nod at me.

"Yeah… Amy, how would you like a job?"

I'm not even sure what to say. I do really need a job, but do I want to work for Dex? It would just be one more thing that he could hold over my head and that's the last thing I need right now. No matter what, it's very nice of him to offer.

"Great," Dex says, handing the folder back to me. "Now, take this to the copy room and get six copies made and bring them back here."

I don't know what to say… I guess I have a job.

"Oh, the copy room is in the next building over."

Dex turns, walks away and Spencer follows him. I guess I'm working for Dex.

I walk to the next building over, drawing the eyes of security as I do, and I wander around until I find the copy room. I'm sure that Dex probably wanted the copies right away, but I'm feeling a little overwhelmed by the whole situation. When I got up this morning I never thought that I would be the assistant to a major Hollywood director and I would be on a movie set. I know that making copies isn't exactly making it big, but for some reason I feel good about it.

It hits me… Dex has been really generous so far and I should be able to make enough working for him to easily get back to Salem in time for school. Heck, if he pays me enough, I might even be able to fly back to Salem instead of taking a bus, which would be really nice.

I finish making the copies and head back to give them to Dex. He's not on the set anymore, but Spencer is there. Ugh. He's talking to some cute girl who looks like an actress. I can see him trying to put the charm on and it's clearly working. I feel a twinge of jealousy… it's strange…. I can't explain it. I don't like Spencer, so why would I feel jealous of that girl?

I clear my throat and draw Spencer's attention. I know he's talking to me, but I'm focused on the girl and the dirty look she's giving me. I just smile at her until she finally turns away.

"Are you even listening to me?"

"Nope."

"Dex is in a meeting with a producer right now and he wants you to bring the scripts to him."

"Where is he?"

Spencer shakes his head, probably because he already explained all of this to me, but I wasn't listening. The smile never fades from his face.

"Just go out that door," he says, pointing. "And take a right and you'll see his trailer, it has his name on the door."

"Thanks."

I walk by him and out the door before he can say

anything else. I'm not about to fall into his trap.

Spencer was right, it's not possible to miss the trailer. It's the biggest trailer I've ever seen and I can't even imagine what kind of truck is needed to tow it. I knock on the door and wait.

"Come in," Dex says, his voice coming from inside.

I open the door and walk inside. It's amazing. I don't even notice the two men sitting on the couch. Not only is it huge inside, but the quality of everything is nicer than anyone's house I've ever been to, apart from Dex's.

"Amy?"

I nod and turn my attention to Dex. Sitting on the couch next to him is an older man, maybe in his early sixties. His white hair is thinning and his eyes look tired, but there's something about him that makes me want to look at him as if he's the most important man in the room.

I walk over to them and hand the folder to Dex and smile. He smiles back.

"You can just take a seat over there," Dex says, pointing at a comfy looking chair.

I sit down and take out my phone, unsure if I'm supposed to be listening or not, to what the two men are saying.

"I don't care, Erin," Dex says.

"I care… I'm the executive producer and I'm not just going to let you recast the female lead because she's being difficult."

"She's not just being difficult and you know that. I could handle that, I've dealt with plenty of difficult actors… she's trying to say that she's had other offers to shoot this month and they are paying better."

"So… then we pay her more."

"She agreed to do this movie for forty thousand, and she signed a contract. I say we make her do it," Dex says.

My eyes widen. It's amazing to me that someone would be upset about making that kind of money, but I guess that's not very much for an actor.

"And what happens if we don't pay her and she walks?" Erin says.

Dex is silent for a time. I glance up and see that he's deep in thought, trying to work out a solution to appease Erin.

"We let her walk… I don't even care at this point."

Erin scoffs and stands up from the couch.

"Really, Dex? She wants what, a million? Fine we pay it to her. Do you have any idea how far behind schedule it would put us if she walks? We would have to do a whole new round of auditions and shut down production until we find a replacement. I can't afford that, I need this movie to make money."

Dex stands up and walks over to a desk.

"How much did you put in? One point five?"

"Yeah, why?"

Dex starts writing something. I didn't want to eavesdrop on their conversation, but now I can't stop watching them. Dex rips something and turns around to Erin and hands him a piece of paper.

"There's two, now get out of my trailer and let me make my movie."

Erin has a shocked look on his face, but he takes the check from Dex and puts it in his pocket and heads toward the door.

"Good luck, you're gonna need it," Erin says.

Dex glares at the back of the older man's head as he walks out of the trailer. Dex sits back down on the couch, visibly exhausted.

"Can you get me a drink, Amy?"

"Sure," I say, standing up from the chair and walking toward the fridge. "What would you like?"

"Something strong."

I stand in front of the open fridge. I have no idea what that means… all I see in here is bottles of water, sports drinks and some juice.

"I…."

"Sorry," he says, pointing to a cabinet next to the fridge. "Whiskey is in there and just grab some ice out of the freezer."

I find a glass in one of the cabinets and fill it halfway full of ice before finding the whiskey. I have no idea how much to pour, so I just fill the glass halfway. I walk over to Dex and hand it to him.

"Thanks."

I stand in front of him for a few seconds while he sips on his drink and then I sit down on the other side of the couch.

"Do you think I did the right thing?"

"What?"

"Paying off Erin… and then letting our female lead walk. Did I mess up?"

"I have no idea… I know nothing about movies."

Dex shrugs, takes a long swallow of the drink and sets it down on the coffee table.

"If you ask Erin, neither do I."

I still have no idea what I'm supposed to say to Dex. He looks a little worried and stressed out, something that I've not seen before.

There's a knock on the door of the trailer. I look over at Dex and he nods. I get up from the couch, open the door and I'm greeted by the smiling face of Spencer.

"Yo, Dex, can I come in?"

"Yeah."

I stand aside and Spencer comes in, walks by me and sits next to Dex on the couch.

"What's up with Erin? He just stormed off the lot and told me 'Good luck, you're gonna need it'."

"Nicole is demanding a million or she's going to walk. Erin insisted we pay her, so I gave him his investment back plus five hundred."

Spencer looks surprised. He gets up from the couch and grabs a bottle of water from the fridge, more as a distraction and to give himself time to think.

"Well... what now?"

"We let Nicole walk. The three of us, and Erin to an extent, took on this project because we wanted to make a great film. Erin and I were financing the whole thing and he was banking on it to make money. I don't care if it makes money, I want it to be special... I want it to blow everyone away who sees it... I want it to change their lives."

Spencer nods as he listens to Dex and then takes a long drink of water.

"You know I'm on board one hundred percent and I trust you completely, man."

"Thanks, Spencer. I'm glad someone understands what we're trying to do."

"What about the scenes with Nicole that we shot already?" Spencer says.

Dex picks up his drink, finishes the rest of it in one swallow and holds it up in my general direction. I get up and make him another drink and he doesn't answer Spencer until he's had a sip of it.

"We have to reshoot them. I don't care what it costs, that's what Erin didn't get... I'll spend whatever it takes to make this film."

"Who are you going to get to replace Nicole?"

"I don't know... do you have any ideas?"

Spencer takes another drink of his water and pulls out his phone. He scrolls through his phone for thirty seconds before he puts it back in his pocket.

"Not really. Everyone I can think of is in production already... and I know you can't wait for a couple of months to keep shooting."

Dex finishes his second drink and I start to get up, but he shakes his head at me and I stay put.

"I don't want to suspend production. Let's just deal with Nicole first and then we can figure out what to do."

"She's not going to like it."

Dex starts laughing and Spencer joins in.

"No, she's gonna be pissed," Dex says. "Amy, can you go get Nicole for me? Turn left when you leave my trailer and hers is the second one. She should be in there."

I swallow and nod. This is quite the start to my new job. It's a lot more exciting than working at Burgers-R-Us or the diner in Greenville.

I get up and leave Dex and Spencer and go to find Nicole. I knock on her trailer door, but there's no answer. I knock a second time and still nothing. I knock a third time, but much harder, and the door swings open from the force. Clearly not the same quality of trailer as Dex has.

"Hello?" I say, sticking my head in the door.

There's silence and I get ready to go inside and call out again.

"What?"

It's a woman's voice, shrill with a heavy dose of irritation. Great, just what I need.

"Nicole?"

"What do you want?"

I guess that means she's Nicole. I can see why Dex and Spencer were laughing, she seems difficult and I haven't even met her yet. It's gotta be this city.

"Dex is asking for you, I'm... I'm his assistant, Amy."

"Ugh... tell him I'll be right there."

I head back to Dex's trailer and go inside. Both men look like they are holding their breath, just waiting for Nicole to walk in the door after me.

"She said she'll be right over."

I sit back down in the chair as the guys let out a collective sigh of relief, even though they know it's temporary.

Nicole opens the door a few seconds later, walks in, looks at the couch and turns to me. I quickly jump out of the chair and move to one that's behind her and further from the action, which is just fine with me.

"You wanted to see me?"

"I did."

"Well, I'm assuming that you talked to Erin and decided that you can afford to pay me what I'm worth."

"I did talk to Erin and he's no longer a part of this production. Moving forward it's just me and I've decided that we are going to part ways. You said that your phone has been ringing off the hook with offers and that this film has made it impossible for you to make the kind of money you are worth, so I think it would be best if you did just that."

Nicole stands up, her fists balled at her side.

"Are you kidding me? I know you have the money to pay me, you cheap son of a bitch. How much is he paying you, Spencer? I'm willing to bet it's a lot more than forty thousand."

"Twenty, actually," Spencer says.

Nicole shakes her head. I don't think she believes him, but he sounded sincere.

"Nicole, I thought you were on board with making this film, but it's obvious now that you had some kind of other motivation for agreeing to it."

"Whatever, Dex. I'm outta here. Good luck finding someone as good as me who's willing to work for scraps."

Nicole storms out of the trailer and slams the door. The guys are silent for a few moments as they digest what has just happened. Now I can see why they were not looking forward to telling her.

"Well," Dex says, "that went how I thought it would."

Spencer and Dex start laughing. I'm glad they feel so calm about the whole situation. I can't even imagine being in Dex's shoes right now—paying out millions of dollars and risking the entire film all for the sake of art. It's actually kind of admirable.

I feel like for the first time I actually see who the real Dex is. He's not the manipulative guy, who was just being nice to me to clear his conscience by giving me things. No, he's a nice guy who cares about movies and making a really good one, even if he has to risk it all to make that happen.

I wonder if maybe I was wrong about him.

"Let's get some lunch," Dex says.

The three of us stand up and head outside.

"I like the way you think," Spencer says.

"What sounds good?"

We start walking toward the other side of the lot.

"Chinese?" Spencer says.

"I'm good with that. What about you Amy? Do you like Chinese food?"

I'm surprised that Dex is even asking me. I just assumed that they were going to go eat and that I would be doing some kind of work or something while they were gone, that or I was going to have to go get the food and bring it back to them.

"You look so surprised."

"Sorry," I say. "I... Yeah, I like Chinese."

I realize there's no point in explaining my thoughts to them, I'll just sound stupid.

"Just ride the wave, Amy, there's nothing you can do other enjoy yourself and see where it takes you," Spencer says.

I smile at him, but he's looking off into the distance. He's right, I need to just relax. I feel like for the first time in since I've left Salem things are going to be alright. I have a job and I'm sure thousands of girls would kill to be standing in my shoes at this moment.

CHAPTER FOURTEEN

My alarm goes off at six-thirty and I press the snooze twice, finally getting up at twenty to seven. Dex told me last night that I needed to be downstairs at seven so that we could leave for the set. I pushed it to the last minute and quickly got ready.

Dex was standing at the door to the garage, with a smile on his face, when I got downstairs.

"Perfect timing."

I smile back at him as I force myself not to yawn. I'm not happy to be up at this time of day, but it feels good to have a job. We go into the garage and Dex opens the door of a gorgeous red sports car that just oozes sex and money. I get in the passenger seat and run my hand across the tan leather of the dash. It even feels expensive.

"It's beautiful."

Dex lets out a chuckle as he pushes a button on the steering wheel and the engine comes to life with a monstrous roar, which is coming from right behind us.

"It's a Ferrari 458 Italia."

I don't know what that means, but I remember Mitch had a poster of a similar looking car on his wall and I'm pretty sure it was a Ferrari. I was wondering if Dex drove himself around, especially since my mom has Ricardo with her… but now that I'm sitting in his car I don't have to even ask. I can't imagine having someone else drive you around if you could be behind the wheel of this.

Dex opens the garage door and backs the car out. He pulls onto the street in front of the house and goes in the same direction that the hired car took me yesterday.

"Oh, your mom is back by the way. She got in late last night."

Ugh. A part of me was trying to ignore the reality that she was coming back. I'm not sure what to say to Dex and I have a feeling he knows that.

"So," he says. "We didn't talk about it yesterday, but we need to discuss how much I'm paying you."

He's right, he hadn't discussed it and I just kind of assumed that it would be the same if not more than any job I could find, not to mention now I can make money right away.

"Whatever you think is fair," I say.

"Well, my last assistant made twenty an hour… is that alright with you?"

"Yeah, that sounds great."

It's more than I was expecting, that's for sure. I know that if I could get a job at a busy restaurant I could make a lot more than that, but that's a big if and twenty an hour is a lot more than a place like a coffee shop or clothing store would pay me. I smile and for a brief moment forget that I'm going to have to see my mom tonight.

When we get close to where we were yesterday, Dex takes a different road and stops in front of a security gate. The guard waves and raises the barrier. We drive through and park in a spot near the front door of the building. It's a three story glass front building with a large sign that says 'DB Productions'.

We get out of the car and walk through the automatic doors and into the lobby, which is filled with modern furniture, glass and steel. There's a group of twenty or so young women standing in one of the corners of the big open room and they are all watching us as we walk to the front desk.

"Good morning, Mr. Baldwin," the woman behind the counter says.

"Good morning… are those the girls?"

"Yes, sir. Should I send them in or wait?"

"Is Spencer here yet?"

Dex looks down at his watch and then back at the woman.

"Yes, he's waiting in the casting room for you."

"Amazing. Give me five minutes and then send them in."

"Sure thing."

I follow Dex down a wide hallway and through a door that's marked 'Casting'. Spencer is sitting in the chair on my right and he stands up when we walk through the door. He flashes us a perfect smile.

The room isn't what I really expected, although I'm not sure what I was expecting. It's a good sized room, that's not it… it just seems very sparse. There's a long table near the back wall, with three chairs, a video camera on a tripod and that's it.

"Hey, Dex, Amy, how are you?"

I nod, thinking it best not to really say much since I'm just here as Dex's assistant.

"I'm good," Dex says. "Are you ready for this?"

They both laugh as we sit down, Dex in the middle, Spencer on his left and me on his right.

"I just hope we can find someone today," Dex says. "Right now I'm paying the whole production crew to stand around and that's not going to change until we find Nicole's replacement."

I can't even fathom the sheer amount of stress that he's under right now. Other than the brief moment yesterday, when he paid off Erin, he's been completely calm.

There's a knock on the door and Dex turns to me. I

jump up, go open the door and close it behind the girl once she's inside. She walks over to the table, sets a headshot down in front of Dex and takes a few steps back.

He picks up the headshot, looks at it and then looks at the girl for a minute without saying anything. Standing behind her I can see the intensity in his eyes and it's obvious she's starting to feel it, because she's starting to squirm.

"OK, Monica, go ahead and start your monologue," Dex says.

She takes a deep breath and shakes her hands out like she's trying to get loose.

"Thou... know'st the mask... of night is on my face, else would a maiden blush... bepaint my cheek...."

"You can stop there," Dex says.

Her body starts to heave and she puts her head in her hands, turns and runs toward the door crying. I open it just in time and close it behind her while we wait for the next person.

"Yikes," Dex says. "I hope that the next ones are better."

I didn't think she was *that* bad, she just seemed really nervous. I actually feel a little bad for her. Dex sets her headshot to the side and whispers something to Spencer. There's another knock on the door and I open it for the next girl.

She's shaking as she walks by me and toward the table. I already know this isn't going to end well.

~~~

I close the door and turn back toward the table.

"I think it's time for lunch," Dex says. "Amy, can you go tell them not to send any more for the next hour?"

"Sure."

I walk out of the room and head for the front desk so that I can stop them before they send the next girl in. I walk up to the desk and the receptionist turns to me.

"Yes?"

"Dex… I mean Mr. Baldwin would like to take an hour break for lunch."

"Sure thing, Hun," she says, smiling at me.

I head back to the casting room and get back just as Dex and Spencer are walking out. They both have smiles on their faces and seem to be in a good mood. I have a feeling that if I was in their position, I wouldn't be so calm. I would probably be a nervous wreck and I would hire the first girl that walked through the door who could form a semi coherent sentence.

I guess that's why I'm the assistant and they're famous.

"Where should we go?" Dex says.

"Mexican?"

"The place right down the road?"

"Yeah."

"You good with Mexican, Amy?"

I nod my head. I have no preference really, I'll eat anything at this point since I skipped breakfast.

I do feel a little bad for all the girls so far… they've been mediocre at best, but Spencer and Dex seemed to think that most of them were downright awful. It can't be easy for them… if I had to guess, most of them were close to me in age. I just can't imagine moving to L.A. and trying so hard to do something and it not working out, it's gotta be so awful and disheartening. I guess them trying to go after their dreams, even if they fail, is admirable.

"So, Amy," Dex says. "What did you think? Did any of them strike you as an actress?"

"Well, it depends."

"What do you mean?" Spencer says.

"I've seen plenty of awful movies with people who *can't* act, but there they are…."

They both laugh and Spencer pats me on the shoulder.

Something happens when his hand touches me. A weird feeling passes through my body, kind of like when Logan touches me, and I push the thought out of my mind.

The restaurant is only a short walk and they seem to know Dex since they seat him at what they call his 'usual' table.

I look through the menu while Dex and Spencer continue their conversation about the lack of quality acting talent they saw this morning. They both somehow still seem optimistic they will find the right actress for the part.

Our waitress, a young Hispanic girl, walks over to the table and pulls an order pad out of her apron pocket. I'm starting to really like being on this side of the restaurant business. Growing up we never really could afford to eat out very often and now I'm about to have my second lunch out in as many days. This is a luxury I'm going to miss once I move back to Salem.

"What would you like?"

She looks at me first, so I quickly scan the menu for something I recognize.

"Chicken tacos."

She writes it down on her pad before turning to Dex next.

"Chili rellenos, please."

"Taco salad, for me," Spencer says.

"Anything to drink?"

"I'll just have water," I say.

Dex cringes and shakes his head.

"Oh, sorry, can I have a bottled water?"

She nods. I guess the water here really isn't drinkable.

"I'll take the same," Dex says.

She turns to Spencer and he nods at her to signify the order of a third bottled water. Once she's clear of the table, I turn my attention to Dex in the hope that he can shed some light on the water.

"Don't ever drink the tap water here, it's disgusting," he says.

I turn to Spencer, who nods in agreement. It's weird, I grew up always drinking tap water in Greenville and it was fine and it tasted alright. I could have never fathomed that I would have to drink bottled water every time I was thirsty. I guess that's just another quirk about L.A., like the rude people, that tends to be ignored in an effort to glorify what happens here.

"Is there something wrong with the water?" I say.

Spencer cracks a smile. Our waitress comes back with three bottles of water and some glasses and sets them down in front of us.

"Yes, but your guess is as good as mine when it comes to what's wrong with it," Dex says.

I'm glad they warned me, I've got no desire to try the water anytime soon.

Our waitress comes back with a large tray and sets our plates down in front of us. Mine has a side of rice and beans, both of which look as good as the tacos. She also sets a basket of chips and a cup of salsa in the middle of the table before leaving.

"You'll like the food, it's very authentic," Dex says.

I pick up one of my tacos and bite into it. The flavor combination of the chicken, salsa and cheese explodes into my mouth. Dex was right, I do like it.

The three of us are silent while we eat and I'm the first one done, which pretty much never happens. I guess it was a combination of the great food and skipping breakfast. I'm going to have to start eating before we leave in the morning.

"How was it?" the waitress says, checking on us for the first time since she brought our food.

We all nod and she walks away again. Dex smiles and looks at me.

"The service isn't as good as the food, but that's why we come here. Usually we are talking about work while we eat, so it's not that big of a deal if the service is at the lacking end of the scale."

I smile and take the last drink of my bottle of water. Dex pulls out his wallet and sets his credit card on the table, just like he did at the Chinese restaurant yesterday and the waitress picks it up without ever showing him the bill. It must be nice not to have to even care what a lunch like this costs. I remember on the few occasions that I actually went out to eat with my parents, they would pour over the check before they reluctantly paid.

"Thanks for lunch, again," I say.

"You're quite welcome, it's the least I can do."

The waitress comes back with his card and the slip for him to sign.

"So," Dex says, while signing. "Should we get back and get the rest of these auditions over with?"

"Do you think we are going to find what we are looking for?" Spencer says.

I can sense a little worry in his voice and it makes me wince. For the first time since I've been here I'm actually feeling a little bit of pity for Dex, which is almost unbelievable. I never thought it was possible to feel sorry for someone who had everything and took so much from me. Am I crazy?

"I hope so. If not... well... I'm not sure what I will do."

Spencer slaps Dex on the back and flashes him a big smile.

"You can always go back to making big budget action flicks."

Dex shrugs. He doesn't look very happy about the possibility, but it looks like it's already crossed his mind and he's come to terms with it.

CHAPTER FIFTEEN

I open the door to my room, let out a deep sigh and sit down on my bed. I would have never guessed that listening to young girls audition and then cry when their dreams were dashed could be so exhausting.

After lunch we saw another thirty women, and Dex and Spencer didn't seem happy with any of them. I could see the expression on Dex's face change as the day went on. By the time he cut auditions short at four, he was starting to look a little defeated. Even the drive home in his glorious car didn't seem to cheer him up.

When we got home he said he was going upstairs to decompress a little and he asked me to tell Gina he would be down at six for dinner. She seemed surprised, I guess this wasn't the usual Dex.

I got off my bed, looked out the window and was greeted by a sight that I knew was coming, but I was still dreading with every fiber of my being—my mom was laying next to the pool, in a bikini no less. Why does she think it's OK for a woman her age to be wearing a swimsuit like that? It doesn't even look good....

Ugh. Thinking about actually having to talk to my mom is making me sick. I'm not sure why, it's impossible for her to ruin my life any more than she already has. I would be fine if I never saw her again after what she put Dad and me through.

This is definitely one of those moments where I wish I could drive and had a car, because I would just leave in order to avoid talking to her. I take a deep breath, knowing that it's going to happen sooner or later, no matter what I want. I'm eventually going to have to talk to her.

My phone chirps, a welcome distraction from thinking about my mom, so I pull it out of my purse expecting it to be a text from Logan. It's not, it's from Spencer.

Hey, Amy, I was wondering if you wanted to go out for a cup of coffee or something in a few minutes. I have a couple of things I want to talk to you about. Spencer.

I'm not even sure what to think. I have no idea how he got my number, because I certainly didn't give it to him. Normally I would never agree to see him… I don't want to be in that kind of position. I certainly don't want to lead him on, but right now I'll take any excuse to get out of the house if it means avoiding my mom.

Sure. You need to pick me up though.

Am I doing the right thing? Should I have said no? Probably, but it's too late for that now.

I'll be there in ten minutes.

I get up and go into the bathroom and brush my teeth. I contemplate changing my outfit, but he's already seen me today so it might be kind of weird if I changed to go out for coffee. I toss my phone in my purse and head downstairs.

I pop my head into the kitchen, where Gina is busy cooking.

"I'm going out for a bit… with Spencer."

She turns around and grins at me and nods.

"It's not like that," I say.

"Sure, it's not. Will you be joining your mom and Dex for dinner?"

"Yeah, I can't imagine I'll be gone for more than an

hour, we're just going to get a cup of coffee."

She nods and turns back to her cooking. I get outside just in time for Spencer to pull his black sedan through the gate and hop out.

"You ready?"

I nod as he rushes around the front of the car and opens the front door, waiting for me to get in. I feel my face turning red and I quickly duck into the car. I take a deep breath and calm myself before he climbs back in.

He pulls the car through the gate and turns toward Santa Monica Boulevard.

"So, what did you want to talk to me about?"

"Oh… it's not a big deal. We can just talk about when we get to the coffee shop."

We're quiet for the next couple of minutes as he drives. He turns onto Santa Monica Boulevard and parks in front of the coffee shop where I wanted to get a job. Really? Out of all the coffee shops in L.A., he had to bring me here? Well, the girl didn't recognize me last time, so maybe she won't this time either.

"You want to get coffee *here*?" I say.

He turns to me and gives me an inquisitive look.

"Yeah… why?"

"Never mind."

I shouldn't have said anything. It doesn't really matter, the girl is either going to recognize me or she isn't and I'm not sure why I even care.

We get out of the car, Spencer holds the door of the coffee shop open for me and we go inside. There's a line, not nearly as long as last time I was here, and we wait our turn. I peek over the shoulder of the guy in front of me and see that it's the same girl and she seems quite chipper. When it's our turn I smile at her as I step up to the counter. Her happy expression quickly fades when she recognizes me.

"What do you want?"

"Two lattes and a blueberry muffin," Spencer says.

She turns her attention to him and she no longer looks irritated with me, instead looking amazed that he's standing in front of her. I force myself not to laugh. He pays for our coffee and the muffin and we stand to the side while they make them.

A young guy, who clearly doesn't recognize Spencer sets our drinks and the muffin on the counter.

"Should we have these outside?" Spencer says.

I nod, grab my latte and follow Spencer outside. It's a little warm outside, but I was starting to feel like we were starting to draw a little too much attention from the staff. We sit down at one of the tables outside and I take a sip of my latte.

"So, what did you want to talk to me about?" I say.

He pulls a piece of the muffin off and pops it in his mouth before pushing it toward me. I would love a piece, but I'm still feeling full from lunch.

"I'm good, thanks."

He shrugs, pulls the muffin back and takes another piece off of it.

"I wanted to talk to you about today," Spencer says.

"What about it?"

He takes a sip of his latte before he answers.

"I feel like Dex was a little discouraged. You would know better than me, since you rode in the car with him on the way home. Did you get that sense from him, or am I crazy?"

He's right, but I'm not sure how Dex would feel about me sharing that with Spencer. I guess it's alright….

"Yeah, I think he did seem a little off on the drive home."

"Huh… I mean I know it wasn't an easy day, he's gotta be stressed. I hope that he's OK."

I find myself feeling a little sorry for Dex, which is such a strange feeling, and it's not the first time. If I told myself six months ago that I would be living in the house of a major Hollywood director, working for him and that I felt sorry for him, I would have never believed it.

"Yeah."

We both drink our lattes and Spencer finishes off the muffin before we say anything else.

"Thanks for the coffee."

"Did you like it?"

"Yeah, it was good. I'm not a big coffee drinker, but I liked that."

He smiles and nods. I notice that he glances over his shoulder for the second time in the last couple of minutes.

"Is everything alright?"

"Yeah... I think there's some paparazzi over there."

I crane my neck and look. Sure enough, there are three guys standing just down the street with cameras, taking pictures. Crazy. I never thought that I would live to see paparazzi in real life... and if I did, they wouldn't be taking pictures of me or someone I knew.

"Do you want to get out of here?" Spencer says.

"Sure."

He cracks a smile and we get up from the table. When he said that, I assumed he meant we were going to get back in his car and head back to the house, but we start walking down the sidewalk.

"So, did you think any of the girls today could come close to what Dex is looking for?" I say.

"Not really."

"Really?"

I felt the same way, but I figured maybe he saw something different. He is a famous actor after all and I'm a nobody.

"There were a couple that were borderline, and if anyone beside Dex was the director they would have probably been ready to use one of them, but he's not going to compromise his vision by choosing the wrong actress."

That makes sense. I could tell by Dex's conversation with Erin that he was going to make sure he made the film that he wanted to make.

"What's he going to do?"

Spencer is quiet for the next few minutes as we walk.

"I'm not sure. I have this feeling in my gut that we'll find the right girl for the job."

It's good that he's so optimistic… I just hope that Dex is feeling the same way about it.

"Let's go in here," Spencer says, taking my hand in his and pulling me into a store.

Before I realize it, we are standing in the boutique where I dropped off my resume… and lo and behold, the same two girls are working today. They notice us and their eyes grow wide when they realize who we are. I can see their eyes flick from me, realizing who I am, and then back to Spencer.

"Is there something we can help you find?" the girl on the left says, as she moves from behind the counter and approaches us.

Their suddenly friendliness now that I'm here with Spencer is irritating. It's amazing to me how much they made fun of me when I came in alone and now they look like they will do anything for us… well for Spencer at least.

"We're just looking."

"Certainly… just let us know if there's *anything* that we can help you with."

I raise my eyebrow at the emphasis on the 'anything' and I turn to Spencer who doesn't seem fazed by it. I wonder if this is the sort of treatment he gets on a regular basis.

"Thanks."

Spencer turns toward one of the clothing racks and starts to browse the shirts hanging from it. I stand next to him and look, starting at the other end.

"What was that about?" he says, leaning closer to me.

"What do you mean?"

"They gave you a strange look, like they knew you or something. Have you been here before?"

I'm surprised that he noticed that in the seconds that they had their eyes on me.

"Yeah... I actually came here to apply for a job."

He pulls a shirt off the rack, looks it up and down and then puts it back.

"Huh, well... I'm glad they didn't hire you."

"Yeah?"

"Yeah."

"Why?"

"Because, I think you're going to do great as Dex's assistant, the pay's much better, I'm sure, and the movie business is a blast."

He's right about the pay and it's probably a blast if you're Spencer. I'm sure he makes a lot of money and has access to anything he could ever want... which is nothing like being an assistant.

Spencer, done looking at the rack, turns and points at the front window. I look and see the same paparazzi that were taking pictures of him at the coffee shop.

"They sure like you," I say.

"I think they like making money."

He walks over to a display of bikinis against the back wall. I glance at the girls, who are watching our every move from behind the counter, and walk over to Spencer.

"Do you need a new bikini?" I say, being a little bit of a smart ass since he's looking at a display that only has women's swimwear.

"No, but you do."

His voice is flat and he sounds completely serious. I try to swallow, but my throat is so dry that I almost choke. He has instantly removed the last sliver of doubt from my mind about whether or not he noticed that my bra was see-through when I got out of the pool. I feel my face getting hot and I look away from him.

"Here, try this on."

Spencer pulls a bikini set off a rack and extends it to me.

"I'm good, I don't need a swimsuit."

He grabs my hand and puts the hanger in it.

"Yes, you do. Now go try it on."

I turn and walk toward the back corner of the store to the dressing room. I glance at the girls as I walk by, but their attention is consumed by Spencer. So crazy. I can't imagine what it's like to have people look at you like that.

I get in the changing room and take a deep breath as I look at myself in the mirror. Am I really doing this? I should be back home right now, getting ready to have dinner with Dex and my mom, but I would rather hang out with Spencer.

I try on the bikini and spin around in the mirror. It fits perfectly... I have no idea how Spencer could have known what size I wear. It's black, with white polka dots and the soft fabric feels amazing against my skin. I glance at the price tag and I shriek.

"Is everything OK in there?" Spencer says.

"Yes... I'm fine."

I look down at the price tag again, making sure that I wasn't seeing things. How can a bikini cost ninety-seven dollars?

"Are you going to come out and let me see it?"

"No."

I quickly change out of it and put it back on the hanger.

"Was I supposed to leave it in the dressing room?"

"Did it fit?" he says.

"Yes... but I'm not going to buy it."

"I know, I am."

"What?"

"I'm buying it, for you."

"I can't let you do that."

He takes the bikini from my hands and sets it down on the counter and comes back with a gray dress and a pair of black pumps.

"Try these on."

"I can't let you buy me anything."

"You can, and you will. Now go try this on."

I reluctantly take the dress and the pumps and go back into the dressing room. I can tell that he's not going to take no for an answer. I'm hesitant about letting him buy me anything… I don't want him to get the wrong impression.

I put the dress on and look at myself in the mirror. It's really nice, much nicer than anything I own. The dress is a sleeveless, knee-length and has a belt around the waist. The top is fitted and the bottom is flared. It fits perfectly. I don't want to take it off. I pick up the shoes, which are also my size, and lean my hand against the wall as I put them on.

"How does it fit?"

"Perfectly."

I don't dare look at the price tag.

"Come out so I can see."

I hesitate… I don't know why, but a part of me doesn't want to let Spencer see me like this. I open the door and walk out into the store. The girls turn and look at me, the same surprised look is on their faces as when we came in.

"It looks fantastic," Spencer says.

He's right… it does. I hope that someday I'll be able to actually afford to own clothes like these. I turn and start walking back to the dressing room.

When I come out, wearing my clothes, which suddenly feel very… ordinary, Spencer is at the counter talking to the women. He turns and flashes me a smile.

"Where's the dress?"

"I left it in the dressing room. Isn't that where I'm supposed to leave it?"

He nods to one of the girls and she hurries off and comes back with the dress and the shoes and sets them on the counter next to the bikini. I also notice a gray shoulder bag that matches the dress, on the counter.

"I…."

Spencer turns to me and smiles.

"Please, just let me buy this as a thank you for what you're doing for Dex."

I fail to see how my working for Dex, as his assistant, makes me deserving of such a reward... but I'm starting to get the impression that trying to talk some sense into Spencer is a losing battle and I might as well just let him buy me the clothes. I have a feeling this might come back to haunt me, but I'm not sure what I can do other than to flat out reject his offer and I don't think that would help my situation with Dex now that he's been gracious enough to give me a job.

"Alright."

His face lights up and he pulls his wallet out of his back pocket and puts a credit card on the counter. One of the girls rings everything up and puts it all in a large bag.

"Your total is seven hundred and forty-six dollars and twelve cents."

"Wonderful. What a bargain," Spencer says.

Holy crap. Seven hundred dollars?!? I can't even wrap my mind around buying that much stuff for that kind of money.

"Spencer?" I say.

He holds up his hand as the girl runs his card and hands it back to him along with the slip to sign. He signs it and hands me the bag as he puts his card back in his wallet. I still feel like I'm in a little bit of shock as we walk out of the door.

I look around when we get outside and the paparazzi seem to be gone. We head back in the direction of the car and I feel a sense of relief pass through me... I don't think I could take him spending a single penny more on me.

"That was very kind of you, Spencer, you didn't have to do that."

"I know, but I wanted you to have something nice to wear to work... for tomorrow."

"What's tomorrow?"

He turns to me and winks while flashing me a huge

smile.

"What? Is something happening tomorrow that I don't know about?"

"You'll just have to wait and see," he says.

I don't like the sound of that. I have a feeling that he's going to do a wonderful job of doing something stupid that will embarrass the crap out of me and I'm not looking forward to it. The problem is that he's just bribed me and I can't do a thing about stopping him. Fantastic.

I guess tomorrow is going to be a rather interesting day.

CHAPTER SIXTEEN

When Spencer pulls his car out the parking spot he makes no effort to turn around.

"Where are we going?"

"You'll see."

"I told Gina that I would be back to have dinner with them… it's getting to be about that time."

"It's fine, I texted Dex while you were trying on clothes to let him know that you weren't going to be there for dinner."

"What?"

Spencer is silent for the next couple of minutes, probably because he could sense the irritation in my voice. I get that he's trying to be nice… but whisking me away without my permission is not making me a happy girl.

He pulls the car over and turns off the engine.

"I'm sorry, I should have asked you first. I just… I figured that since you're new here it would be nice for you to be able to get out of the house and just have a little fun. I don't know why you're here, but you don't seem happy to be living with Dex. I can see it in your face and in your eyes. I was just trying to be a good friend."

He starts the car and turns it around and we start back

toward the house. Now I just feel like an ass. Is it possible that he was just doing that? Trying to be a friend since he knew I wasn't happy here?

"I'm sorry. Now I just feel bad."

"It's alright, I get it."

I have so many thoughts swirling around in my head that it's hard to make sense of any of them. I do want a friend, but at the same time I'm leaving in a couple of weeks and I don't know how Logan would feel about me hanging out with Spencer. It's a mess.

"It's not that simple."

"What is it then?"

"I...."

I drop my head into my hands as I start to cry. I just want things to be easy, I never asked for any of this. Is all of this some kind of punishment? How am I supposed to feel good about anything in life after what's happened?

Spencer pulls the car over and puts his hand on my shoulder.

"You can tell me anything."

He says that, but I doubt someone like him wants to hear about my stupid problems. There's no way I'm going to lay all that on him.

"I want to know what's going on. Sometimes it helps to talk about it."

I take a deep breath and force myself to stop crying. I dry the last of my tears with the sleeve of my shirt and look over at Spencer. I can tell by the look in his eyes that he's telling the truth and really does care what's happening in my life. He smiles at me and runs his hand over my shoulder.

"Well," I say. "If I'm going to talk to you about me, and I still don't understand why you would waste your time on that, I think we should talk somewhere that's not your car on the side of this busy road."

He cracks a knowing smile and pulls out of the parking spot. He takes a series of turns, which leaves me hopelessly lost again. Spencer drives in silence, which is fine with me since I'll soon be talking his ear off and telling him my problems.

Spencer pulls the car up in front of a restaurant and someone opens my door for me. I get out and so does Spencer. He hands the valet his keys, opens the door for me and we head inside. The hostess smiles when she sees him and grabs two menus.

"Right this way, Mr. Thomas."

I guess he must be a regular here. I look around as we follow her to the table and I can't figure out what kind of restaurant we are in... nothing seems to give it away which is strange.

She seats us at a booth in the back of the restaurant, far away from the bar. It's fairly quiet which is nice considering our intentions. Hopefully the hostess doesn't get the wrong impression about why we are here.

"Are you hungry?"

"Somewhat," I say.

"Everything here is good."

I browse the menu, which seems to be a combination of every kind of European food. It's kind of strange, but most everything sounds good.

"So," Spencer says, setting down his menu. "What's going on?"

I set my menu down, still not sure what I'm getting and look him in the eyes. There's a softness there, a gentleness almost, that I hadn't noticed before. It's as if his persona, the Hollywood heartthrob, had blinded me to the real Spencer and I was seeing him now for the first time.

It must be a strange feeling, always being looked at as an object of desire—I can't even imagine that.

I spend the next hour filling Spencer in on everything that has happened since the day I got the mistaken rejection letter from State. He stops me every so often to ask a question or to clarify something I've said. It surprises me that he doesn't defend the actions of Dex and he doesn't judge me for any of the choices I made along the way. I tell him everything… except for some reason I leave out the parts that would imply I have sort of romantic relationship with Logan. I don't know why either, it just seemed awkward and I didn't want him to perceive me as a stupid girl who doesn't know the first thing about boys.

"Well… that is quite the story. It almost sounds like something that could be a movie."

"Why do you say that?"

I never thought anything about my life would be interesting to other people.

"It has drama, some romantic elements and loss. It would make a good movie. I would go see it."

He smiles at me and I can tell he's joking, trying to make me feel better. Not to mention I have no idea where he got the notion about romantic elements, especially after I left out the bits about Logan… and there wasn't much to say about Mitch.

I stifle a yawn with my napkin. I'm actually feeling pretty tired, it was a long day after getting up so early. I'm not looking forward to tomorrow being another early day.

"Sorry," I say.

He smiles at me and motions for our server to come over to the table.

"Yes, sir?"

"Can we get the check?"

He nods and hurries off to one of the service stations.

"It's fine," Spencer says, turning back to me. "It was a long day and tomorrow is going to be even longer."

I have a feeling he's right. I got the impression from Dex that tomorrow they have to find someone for the movie or it's going to start costing him a lot of money, not to mention drive his stress level through the roof. I don't envy him, that's for sure.

"Yeah."

Even though I'm exhausted, I'm not in a hurry to get back to the house because I know that I'm going to have to talk to my mom. The conversation I wish I could never have. I'm still furious at her and talking to Spencer tonight has brought all of my feelings back to the surface.

"Are you going to talk to your mom?"

"I don't have a choice. She's there now and I'm sure she'll want to know what I've been doing, so that she can criticize me for something."

"That's what moms are for."

Our waiter drops the check off at the table.

"I seriously doubt your mom was anything like that," I say.

"Like that? She's still that way."

"Really?"

He slides his credit card into the check presenter and stands it up so that our waiter notices.

"Yes. I get a call from her every time there's something about me on the news or on the Internet. I guess she's worried that I'll get caught up in the Hollywood lifestyle and never have a chance to meet a good woman, settle down and have kids."

I would have never imagined that someone so successful, so famous, would have the same kinds of problems in their life as a normal person. It's actually kind of funny and for the first time since we sat down I smile at Spencer.

"That's better."

"What do you mean?"

"You look so pretty when you smile."

I lift my water glass to my lips in an attempt to hide the fact that my face is turning bright red.

The waiter grabs the credit card and pulls a mobile credit card machine out of his apron. He swipes the card, returns it to Spencer and sets the receipt and a pen down on the table.

"Thank you for coming in tonight, Mr. Thomas. We look forward to seeing you again."

"Thanks."

I smile as I watch him happily sign for a dinner that cost what my family would spend on groceries for a week or two. It must be nice not to have to worry about money. Maybe someday that will be me, but I'm not going to hold my breath.

"You ready?"

I nod and smile at Spencer. I'm very grateful that he took me out to dinner and he was right, it did make me feel a little better to talk about the whole thing. It didn't alleviate the stress of talking to my mom, though, which is a little worrisome.

By the time we leave the restaurant and reach the sidewalk, the car is already waiting for us and the valet hands Spencer the keys.

"Thanks," Spencer says, slipping him a tip.

We get in the car and he hangs a U-turn so that we can head back to the house.

"I hope that Dex finds his actress tomorrow," I say.

"I know that he will."

"Yeah? How so?"

"I just know who's coming in for an audition tomorrow and she's perfect for the part."

"Who is it? Anyone I would know of?"

"Yeah, but I want it to be a surprise… not even Dex knows she auditioning."

I wonder who it could be. I decide not to press Spencer anymore, not after everything he's done for me today. It's not like I won't find out tomorrow.

When we get back to the house I get out and Spencer reaches into the back seat to get my bag of clothes and hands it to me.

"Thanks again, you really didn't have to buy me all this stuff."

"No problem. Just don't forget… wear your new outfit tomorrow."

"I won't forget."

It's kind of a little dressy for an assistant, especially

since Dex is usually dressed down, but who am I to argue with Spencer seeing as how he bought it for me.

"Take care," he says.

"You too."

I walk up to the front door and take a deep breath. You can do this, Amy, just try to be calm and don't let her upset you.

I open the door and walk inside, pausing to listen for voices, but the house seems quiet. I head upstairs, not wanting to linger just in case my mom is down here. As I walk by the hallway to the master suite, I hear voices. I stop and listen… I can't tell what they're saying, but they sound upset.

I know that I should just go to my room, it's the smart thing to do, but I can't help myself. I slowly walk down the hall, trying not to make any noise. As I get closer I can start to pick up words from the conversation, but it's not until I'm a foot away from the door that I can hear exactly what they are saying.

"I just can't believe it!" Mom says.

"Why?"

"Why? I'll tell you why. She doesn't deserve it… that's why, she's so ungrateful to be here!"

"She'll come around… but not if we don't help her."

"Ugh!"

"Come on," Dex says. "It's just a job… she needs the money and I needed an assistant."

"Fine, but don't say I didn't warn you when you realize how lazy and incompetent she is."

"She's an assistant, not a brain surgeon."

"Whatever… I'm going to get a drink."

I turn around and sprint toward my room, opening the door just as I hear the door to their room open. I close my door as silently as possible and press my ear against it. I can hear her footsteps as she walks by my room and toward the stairs. When the sound disappears, I finally take a deep breath and retreat into my room.

I put away the bag of clothes that Spencer bought for me and sit down on my bed. I take my phone out of my purse and I'm greeted with a text message from Logan.

How was your first day as a big shot?

It brings a smile to my face to hear from him after today.

It was good, I watched a bunch of girls audition. How was your day?

I don't get a response from Logan, but I'm not that surprised. He could be at a meeting right now, so I get ready for bed. I check my phone after brushing my teeth and changing into my pajamas, but there's still no message from him. I was hoping to talk to him tonight and I probably could have if I hadn't gone out shopping and to dinner with Spencer. Hopefully I'll get a chance to talk to Logan on the phone tomorrow, I miss the sound of his voice.

I get under the covers and stare at my phone, expecting it to light up with a text from Logan at any moment. I resist the pull of sleep, but I eventually can't keep my eyes open any longer and give in.

CHAPTER SEVENTEEN

There's a knock on my door as I slip my second shoe on.

"Coming."

I grab my phone and my bag and head for the door. It feels strange to be wearing a dress to go to work, but I like how I look in it and it's crazy comfortable.

I pull my door open, expecting to see Dex… but it's my mom instead. The smile quickly fades from my face as I look into her eyes. I was really hoping that I would be able to leave this morning without seeing her. I know that putting it off isn't going to make it go away, but first thing in the morning isn't ideal.

"I have to go to work."

I take a step toward her, but she doesn't move.

"We need to talk."

"I'm supposed to get a ride with Dex."

She raises her eyebrow. She knows that I'm trying to avoid talking to her.

"I already told Dex that I needed to talk to you this morning."

So much for using work to get out of talking to her.

"So, what do you need to talk to me about?"

"Let's go sit down, I don't want to just stand here."

I nod and follow her downstairs and into the living room. She sits in a large chair and I sit across from her on the couch. I glance at the clock on the wall as I wonder how late for work I'm going to be. I hope that Dex isn't mad… and I hope I get there in time to see the audition that Spencer was talking about last night.

"I don't think that it's a good idea if you work for Dex," she says.

"What does Dex think?"

She glares at me and clears her throat. I can see the fire in her eyes as she tries to stay calm. Who is this woman? Is she really even the same person that raised me? She certainly doesn't look or act like the school teacher from Greenville. I still can't believe she's changed so much in such a short time.

"I don't think it's a good idea."

"Right… and what does Dex think about me working for him?"

"He seems to think that you'll do a fine job as his assistant."

I'm still a little surprised that they had an argument about it last night. I can't imagine Dex, a guy I hardly know, sticking up for me.

"So why are we having this conversation?"

"Just because you're almost eighteen doesn't mean you can take that tone with me. Don't forget, I'm still your mother."

I so badly want to scream at her and tell her how everything is her fault. She gave up the right to tell me what to do when she ran off with Dex and left me and Dad behind.

"I don't see why you care if I work for Dex."

"I care because I don't want him to feel obligated to employ you. He's not going to want to fire you if you do a bad job."

Does she really think I'm a lazy worker? She's the one who's left working behind to lounge around and spend

Dex's money without a second thought.

"If I suck at being an assistant, then he can fire me... I don't care. I'm leaving in a couple of weeks anyway."

"And where are you planning to go?"

"Back to Greenville and then to Salem. I have to get back and take care of the house before school starts."

"Take care of the house?"

"Yeah... I guess I've gotta pack up whatever I want to keep and get the house ready to sell."

I hadn't really thought about it before this moment, but I guess I can pay for school using the money from the sale of the house and that way I can focus on school and not have to worry about working at the same time. It should make things a little easier.

"What makes you think you get to do that?"

"What do you mean?" I say.

"You can't sell the house... I own it."

I'm confused. She left, which means that the house became my dad's and when he died it should have become mine. At least that's how it should work....

"But... you left...."

"So? I never divorced your father, so the house is still mine... along with everything in it. You are not to set foot in that house again or I will have you arrested."

I can tell she's serious and will call the cops. What a bitch. I hate her so much. I can't wait to just get out of here. I don't even really care about the house, it's just one less thing to think about.

"Fine, whatever," I say, as I stand up. "Can I go now?"

She just looks at me and doesn't answer. I guess that means she's done with me, for now at least.

I walk out of the room and into the kitchen to look for Gina. She's standing over the stove cooking what smells like bacon, toast and eggs.

"Good morning, Ms. Amy. Would you like some breakfast?"

"No thanks, Gina. I was actually wondering if you

happen to know if Ricardo is around. I need a ride to the studio."

She beckons for me to come closer.

"Mr. Baldwin told Ricardo to wait outside for you."

"Thanks, Gina. I'll see you later."

"Have a good day, Ms. Amy. You look very pretty today, by the way."

"Thanks, Spencer bought this for me last night."

She raises her eyebrow and I let out an embarrassed laugh.

"I hope you have a good day, too," I say.

I head outside and Ricardo is there, standing next to the rear passenger door. He opens the door and closes it once I'm in. He gets in the car and pulls out of the driveway and starts driving in the general direction of the studio.

I hear my phone chirp from inside my purse, so I pull it out with the hope that it's Logan and I'll get to text with him for at least a few minutes before I reach the studio. The text isn't from Logan though... it's from Spencer.

Hey, where are you? We are about to start auditions.

I had to talk to my mom this morning, so I'm on my way right now.

Oh... I hope that everything went alright. We can talk about it later if you want. See you soon.

Huh. I have a feeling he was being genuine, but I can't imagine talking to him more about my problems. I kind of figured by this point he would be sick of hearing me talk about my boring life. Last night sort of feels almost unreal... did I really have dinner with Spencer Thomas and he sat there listening to me complain for an hour? Life is crazy sometimes... I never know what will happen next.

I spend the rest of the ride to the studio in silence, thinking that maybe I should text Logan... but I know he'll text me when he gets the chance. I'm really looking forward to getting back to Salem so that I never have to think about the time difference and what he might be doing.

When we get to the studio, Ricardo pulls the car up to the front and gets out to get my door for me.

"Thank you."

He just nods and I think he almost smiles. I turn and walk into the lobby, which once again has a group of girls waiting to audition. I walk up to the counter and smile at the same woman who was working yesterday.

"They are waiting for you," she says.

"Thanks."

I walk down the hall toward the casting room and on my way pass a young girl with a dejected look on her face. I guess auditions already started. I knock on the door and walk in. Dex and Spencer are sitting at the table and they both smile at me as I close the door behind myself.

"Good morning," I say.

"Good morning," they say in unison.

"That's a nice dress," Dex says.

"Thank you…."

I want to tell him that Spencer bought it for me, but there is a knock on the door. Dex nods at me and I turn and open the door. A young woman walks through, glances at me briefly and walks over to the table and sets down her headshot.

"Hey, Jen, how are you?" Dex says.

"Good. How have you been?"

"I'm going a little crazy trying to fill this part, but other than that I'm good. How's your dad?"

"He's good, just working a lot."

I wonder who she is… it seems like she must know Dex from somewhere. Not to mention their conversation has a very informal tone to it.

"So, Jen, I need to say this before you start… I just want you to know that I'm not going to give more consideration for the part because of my professional relationship with your dad… this is a business and I need to pick the person who I think is best for the role."

"I understand."

"Good… you can start your monologue whenever you're ready."

She takes a deep breath, shakes out her arms and rolls her neck in a circle.

"Look, I don't know what to tell you… you can't put this on me. We didn't have a choice… your job forced this move and it's not my fault that I had to stay behind for a couple of months. You can't blame me for you not being able to not keep your hands off every girl that bats her eyes at you."

She puts her hands on her hips and shakes her head back and forth.

"No, I'm not going to calm down… you need to figure out what it is you want in life, because I'm not going to put up with this kind of shit anymore. Do us both a favor and don't call me until you sort yourself out and actually have enough time to really think about if we should be together."

She stops talking and takes a step back to let them know she's done. It was shorter than most of the monologues we heard yesterday, but there was a passion in her voice that had been absent from all of the other girls that had auditioned. I don't claim that I know much about making movies, but I would say that she was the best one so far.

I close my eyes and I can picture her being in a movie. This must have been the girl that Spencer was talking about. I wonder if Dex was as impressed by her audition as I was.

"Thank you, Jen," Dex says.

"I appreciate you letting me audition."

He smiles at her and leans over to Spencer and whispers something into his ear. Spencer nods, looks at me and then whispers something into Dex's ear.

"So," Dex says, "we have some more girls already waiting to audition, but I would say that it's pretty safe to say that you're in the front running for the part… you can expect us to call you in the next day or two when we've made our decision."

She nods, turns and walks toward the door. I smile at her and hold it open for her and then close it behind her while we wait for the next girl.

"Can we pause the auditions for a minute?" Spencer says.

"Why?" Dex says.

"I want to talk about a girl that I wanted to have audition."

"Is she here?"

"Yeah, she's here."

"What does she look like? Amy can go get her."

Spencer pauses, looks at me and flashes me a smile.

"I want to talk about it before she comes in."

"I know you're up to something," Dex says. "Alright… Amy, could you please go let them know to pause auditions please?"

I nod and walk through the door. There is already a girl walking down the hall with a headshot in her hand.

"Excuse me?" I say.

She looks up at me and stops.

"Are you heading into casting?"

"Yes," she says, her voice shaking.

I can already tell she's not going to do well and I'm sure my delaying her isn't going to help.

"They need to take a short break, so if you could please go sit back down… I'll let you know when they're ready again."

A look of relief passes over her face and I wonder if she doesn't really want to be here. Perhaps it's the dream of her mother… that her daughter will be a famous actress.

I walk up to the front desk and smile at her.

"They need a few minutes to talk something over."

She nods and smiles at me.

"Just let me know when they're ready again," she says.

"I will... I got the impression it shouldn't be very long."

She smiles at me again and I turn to go back to the room. I'm not sure if they wanted me in the room for the conversation, but I assume they don't care since they didn't say anything about it.

I open the door and walk in. They are talking and I can sense the tension in Dex's voice.

"I get what you're saying... she does have the look... but I just don't know if it's a good idea."

I close the door and they both turn to me. A chill passes through my body as I get the feeling that I'm intruding on their conversation.

"Did you want me to wait outside?" I say.

"No, come in," Dex says.

"Just trust me on this," Spencer says.

Dex turns back to him and looks long and hard at the young man.

"Fine...."

"Come over here, Amy," Spencer says.

I walk over to the table and he hands me a piece of paper.

"This is dialogue from the script. Can you please read all of the lines that are highlighted? I'm going to read the other lines so that it sounds like a conversation."

"Sure...."

"I just want to see how it sounds... I'm not so sure about this part of the script." Spencer says.

Dex turns his head and shoots Spencer an irritated glance. Weird... they usually seem to agree about pretty much everything. I guess maybe I haven't been around them enough to get the whole picture.

I take a couple of steps back from the table and clear my throat before reading the first line.

"I just don't get it... why are you so opposed to us being together? We make sense. That's all there is to it."

"Why would you think we make sense? We're terrible for each other," Spencer says.

"What?!?"

"You know we are."

I take a deep breath as instructed by the script, trying not to over exaggerate.

"You're right," I say. "You're right. We aren't good for each other, but that doesn't stop me from wanting to be with you any less."

"Do you really think we could make this whole thing work?"

"Yes… I know we can."

Spencer looks up from his sheet and smiles at me before delivering his next line.

"How can you be so sure about… anything?"

"I'm not sure about anything in life… other than us."

I flip the page and wait for Spencer to read his dialogue, but when I look up Dex and Spencer are just looking at each other.

"Thanks, Amy," Dex says. "Can you give us a minute?"

"Sure. Do you want me to send in the next girl?"

"No… we'll come get you."

Weird. Who am I to judge? It must have something to do with the conversation that I walked in on. It seems like with each passing moment that Dex is becoming more and more consumed with trying to find the perfect girl for his movie.

I lean against the wall and take my phone out my purse while I wait. I half expect to see a text from Logan waiting for me, but there's nothing. I make a mental note to text Jess later, to give her my new number and see if she's seen Logan lately… it's just not like him to not text me.

The door opens and Spencer pokes his head out and nods for me to come back in. I toss my phone back in my bag and follow him.

"Are you ready for the next girl?" I say.

Dex smiles at me and shakes his head.

"We already found the perfect actress for the part."

I feel relieved for Dex... I know how much this means to him and even though this only my third day working for him, I'm starting to feel a real connection to being a part of this movie. I could have never imagined my life heading in this direction.

"Who is it?"

They are both quiet and just stare at me. I glance over my shoulder wondering if maybe there was someone else in the room... but it's just me.

"It's you," Dex says. "I want you to star in my movie opposite Spencer."

Is this really happening? I don't even know what to say.... It's the dream of pretty much every girl to be an actress, so I guess I can't complain, but I didn't see this coming.

"Say something," Spencer says.

He has a big goofy grin on his face and it's all starting to make sense. That's why he bought me the dress yesterday and told me to wear it today... I'm the girl he thought would be perfect for the part... the girl that was going to be a surprise audition for Dex.

I open my mouth to say something, to say anything, but I can't speak. Spencer starts to laugh and Dex smiles at me.

"Congratulations," Dex says.

I take a couple of deep breaths and finally get a hold of myself. I still can't believe it, though.

"Thank you."

"I'm glad that I listened to Spencer... he was being very insistent that you were perfect for the part and I was feeling sort of stuck and ready to choose Jen. She was good, I'll give her that... but you... you're perfect."

I look over at Spencer and he winks at me. It's amazing to have Dex give me this opportunity... I guess I was wrong about him.

"Now what?" I say.

"Now… now we celebrate… because tomorrow you're going to work harder than you ever have in your entire life," Dex says.

A couple of days ago I would have never believed that working on a movie could be hard work, but after spending a couple of days as Dex's assistant I knew what he was saying was true. It's going to hard work… and I don't care.

"What did you have in mind?" Spencer says.

"I was thinking we could go out to dinner… maybe at *Magnifique.*"

"Oooh, fancy," Spencer says.

I can't tell by the playful tone in his voice if he's being serious about it being fancy or if he's mocking Dex.

"I think today's developments warrant it."

"Does that mean you're paying?"

Dex laughs and shakes his head. I smile as the guys stand up and walk toward me. I turn around, open the door and we head out. We stop at the front desk on the way out, as the room full of girls turns and looks at us.

"Please let them know that auditions are now closed… we found our girl."

"Absolutely, Mr. Baldwin."

"Thanks."

As we walk to the door, even before she delivers the bad news, I can see a dejected look on the face of every single girl in the room. I feel a little bad for a brief moment, but the moment we step outside I forget it all. I'm going to be in a movie!

CHAPTER EIGHTEEN

On the way home from the restaurant Dex drives in silence. I have a feeling that we're both thinking about the same thing... how to tell Mom. I'm pretty sure Dex doesn't know that I heard them arguing, but since I do it puts a twist on it. I look over at him and can tell he's deep in thought.

"Everything OK?"

He glances over at me and forces himself to smile.

"Yeah... just fine. Why?"

"You looked miles away."

"Just thinking about the film."

Dex is quiet for the next few minutes and I start to get worried. Is he regretting his decision to put me in his movie? Why didn't he say anything earlier? He could have told Spencer that I wasn't right for the part when I was out of the room... heck I didn't even realize at the time that I was auditioning.

"Are you worried about me being in it?"

"No... you're perfect."

I finally breathe again.

"Were you worried about that?" he says.

"Well... yeah... I mean I've never acted before, so I'm

not sure what I was thinking."

"No... I think you're perfect for the part."

It has to be my mom then. It's the only other thing I can think of.

"It's just... I didn't want to tell you about this... but your mom...."

"I know," I say.

Dex turns to me, nods and then looks back at the road.

"You heard us?"

"I did."

Dex lets out a deep sigh. I decide to not mention that I snuck down the hall so that I could listen to exactly what they were saying. I feel a twinge of guilt... but I don't want to upset Dex even more.

"I'm sorry you had to hear that... I really am."

I shrug. Normally I wouldn't care... but all I can think about is the last few days of my mom still living in Greenville and the fights my parents got in. A few days ago I would have blamed Dex for everything that happened... but now I just don't know. I'm starting to feel like my mom is to blame... and maybe Dex didn't know what he was getting himself into.

"It's OK," I say.

"No, it's not. She was concerned about me giving you a job, as my assistant, so I'm trying to figure out a way to convince her that casting you in my film was the right choice. I know it is... but I have to get her to see it, too."

"Do you have to tell her?"

"I mean... she's bound to find out, eventually, but I guess she doesn't need to know right away. Maybe I'll wait a few days and try and come up with a way to tell her."

"Yeah, I know the feeling of hiding something from her."

Dex pulls the car through the gate and into the garage. He turns off the engine and looks over at me.

"Thank you," he says.

"For what?"

"I was starting to feel disheartened by the search for Nicole's replacement, but now... now you've given me a renewed sense of purpose and I'm ready to make this film."

"Good."

I don't even really know how to respond to something like that. I hope that I can do a good job... that I can act good enough to help him make the movie he wants. I never would have thought a couple of days ago that I would be worried about disappointing Dex... it's amazing the twists that life takes sometimes.

We get out of the car and head inside.

"Are you going to want to eat later?" he says.

"I doubt it."

"Alright... well... I'm going to go see what your mom is doing. If I don't see you later, I'll see you down here at six-thirty."

"Sounds good."

Dex smiles, turns and walks toward the kitchen. I head up the stairs, steadying myself on the handrail as I walk. I'm still trying to get the hang of wearing pumps... I can't believe there're women that walk around in these all the time. Crazy.

When I get to my room, I change into sweats and sit down on my bed. I pull out my phone and my heart sinks when I see there's still no message from Logan. I think about texting him again... but I don't want to bother him if he's busy. Maybe something is going on with football.... I just hope everything's alright and he's OK. I decide to text Jess instead.

Hey, it's Amy, new number again. How are you doing?

I'm good! I was wondering what happened... I thought maybe you got caught up in the Hollywood lifestyle and forgot about your friends back here in Salem.

She brings a smile to my face, just like pretty much every single time I talk to her. I do miss Jess... that's for sure.

Nah… just been very busy and some super exciting stuff has happened. I don't want to tell you about it though until I tell Logan.

Oooh… does it have anything to do with Spencer?

I guess it does… I mean he got me the audition by convincing Dex that I was right for the part, but I don't think that's what Jess was referring to.

No, it doesn't… it has to do with a new job I got.

Oh… well, that's not all that exciting.

I know she's going to feel differently when I actually tell her what the job is.

Yeah… yeah… not all of us are as exciting as you.

Nope, you're all boring. So… when are you still coming back to Salem right after your birthday?

Shit.

I hadn't even thought to ask Dex about how long the movie shoot was going to last. I can't imagine it being done before my birthday. Crap, it probably won't even be done before school starts. What am I going to do?

My phone chirps and I look down, expecting to see a text from Jess or maybe even Logan… but it's a text from Spencer.

Turn on channel 47.

What?

Turn on channel 47… like right now… you'll want to see this, I promise.

Confused as to what it could possibly be, I hop off my bed and go to the game room. I close the door behind myself and turn on the TV. I manage to find channel forty-seven, which is showing a commercial. While I wait for the show to come back on I check the guide, which describes the show as being about celebrity news.

Is there a segment about you or something?

You could say that… just watch.

I roll my eyes and turn my attention back to the TV as the show starts again. Spencer is ridiculous, but at least this will serve as a momentary distraction to my quandary.

The show starts again as the camera pans to a man

sitting behind a desk.

"Welcome back. It appears Spencer Thomas, Hollywood heartthrob, has a new lady in his life... this coming just a few short weeks after his breakup with girlfriend Monica Lister."

The screen flashes to a picture of Spencer with a woman who looks like a model or actress. She's really pretty, I think. I wonder what happened? He seemed so happy and calm since I've known him... I would've never guessed that he just got out of a relationship.

"But now he's been spotted with a new girl... and sources are still trying to figure out who she is."

The screen flashes to a picture of Spencer and me, having coffee.

Crap.

Another picture comes on the screen... this time it's of us leaving the clothing boutique and it looks like I'm laughing.

This is not good.

"Here they are after doing some shopping at a high end Beverly Hills boutique clothing store."

I feel panic filling my body. I want to shut off the TV... to pretend that I never saw this, but I just can't make my arms move to reach for the remote.

"Speculation suggests that perhaps she's the new star of Dexter Baldwin's next film. Not to mention she was spotted leaving *Magnifique*, L.A.'s most exclusive restaurant, with both Baldwin and Thomas."

A video clip of the three of us pops onto the screen and I feel like I can't breathe. Is this really happening?

"Next up...."

Thankful the segment is over, I will my arm to move so I can grab the remote and shut off the TV. I force myself to take a couple of deep breaths. I've gotta get ahold of myself. It was enough to try and think about the movie and my plans to leave here... but now I've got my face plastered all over TV with the implication that I'm dating

Spencer. Ugh.

I pick up my phone and go back to my bedroom. I can't deal with all of this right now. I pull the covers back and climb in. I know it's early… but I feel so overwhelmed by it all. I turn off my phone, pull the covers over my head and try to clear my mind.

As I drift off into sleep all I can think is that I hope all of this was a bad dream and tomorrow will go back to normal.

CHAPTER NINETEEN

There's a knock on my door. I pull the covers back over my head… hoping that it was just my imagination, but there's a second knock… a little louder this time.

"Yeah?"

"Amy, it's Dex… are you feeling alright? It's almost seven."

Great. I feel like I haven't slept and I'm already late. Part of me just wants to stay in bed, crying, for the entire day. I know I can't do that… I can't let Dex down. He's counting on me and it's not his fault that I didn't tell him that my schedule was kind of firm for going back to school.

I get out of bed and open my door. Dex forces a smile across his face and I can tell that he's surprised by my appearance.

"Is everything OK?" he says.

"I didn't sleep very well."

"I can see that."

Dex takes a deep breath and I can see the disappointment on his face. Not in me, but in the fact that he can tell it's just another setback that he doesn't want to deal with.

"Can I have ten minutes?"

He raises his eyebrow and nods. I close the door before he can say anything else and I hurry to get ready.

I toss on some clothes and head out of my room in less than nine minutes, my hair still wet from the shower.

"That was quick," Dex says.

I shrug and walk by him and head downstairs. I already feel bad for making us so late that I'm not going to stand around making small talk. We get in the car and head toward the shooting lot where Dex first hired me as his assistant. It's funny... it's really only been a couple of days, but because of everything that's happened it feels like such a long time ago.

"How are you doing today? Has the fact that you're an actress set in yet?"

"Not really."

Dex laughs and looks over at me with a smile on his face.

"I get that. For most actors it usually doesn't set in until they see themselves on a big screen."

It's actually the last thing I'm thinking about right now. I take a deep breath... there's no time like the present.

"So, Dex... how long will it take to film the parts of the movie that I'll be in?"

He raises his eyebrow and quickly glances at me before turning his focus back to driving in the L.A. traffic.

"I don't know... I would guess it could take four or five weeks. Why?"

Crap. I had a feeling it was going to take longer than I wanted to stay here... not to mention that it'll bump into the beginning of school. Is this an opportunity that is worth missing my first semester of college for?

"I was just wondering."

"Is everything alright? I thought you'd be so excited today... this isn't an opportunity that many people get."

"I am excited... it's just... never mind."

"What is it?"

"Nothing."

"You can tell me, Amy. I want you to be happy, because I want this to be perfect and I want to make sure that you're comfortable."

We sit in silence for the next couple of minutes. I'm still reeling from last night and I'm starting to wonder what I'm doing. Am I really going to act in a movie? Can I really abandon school to do this after everything? I just don't know.

"I… it's hard, Dex. I was planning on leaving in a couple of weeks after my birthday and going back to Salem. School is starting soon, but I do want to be in your movie. I'm just confused and lost I guess."

"I get it, Amy. I truly want you to be in the film, but I don't want you to feel any pressure from Spencer or me. Only you can decide if you want to skip your first semester of school to do this."

I feel a little relieved to know that he doesn't want me to feel pressured to do this. It doesn't change the fact that I have to make a life changing decision and I only have minutes to make it before we get to the lot.

I'm torn. I could go back to school and be with Logan, which is all I've wanted since the moment my mom showed up in Greenville… and I could be happy. At the same time, I could stay here and get to be in a movie, which is an amazing opportunity… the likes of which I might never get again. I'm not sure what to do.

I wish that I had been able to talk to Logan to see what he thinks, but he's still not answering my texts. I'm actually starting to get a little worried. I hope that he's alright. I have a feeling that he would support me in whatever I chose to do, he's just that kind of guy.

What the heck… I'm doing it.

"I do want to be in your movie… school will always be there, but this is a rare chance that you've given me."

Dex flashes me a smile and winks as we pull up to the lot. He parks the car and we get out.

"Are you ready?" Dex says.

"I think so."

"You either are or you aren't."

"I'm ready."

He's right… there's no sense in holding back now.

"Good, now follow me."

We walk to a trailer that has a sign on the door that says 'hair and makeup' and we go inside. It's empty, except for a woman who I would guess is in her mid-thirties. She's wearing a vintage concert tee and has her black hair pulled into a ponytail.

"Hey, Leslie, how are you today?"

"I'm fantastic, Mr. B. I'm ready to get back to work… and I'm glad to be done with Nicole. She was such a pill."

I crack a smile and do everything I can not to laugh.

"This is Amy… Amy, this is Leslie."

"Nice to meet you," I say.

"You too, Hun."

"She's going to do your hair and makeup and when you're done head over to wardrobe. When you're done there come over to stage one and we'll get started."

I just nod as I try to remember everything he's saying. I guess I was expecting some sort of slow start since I'm new to movies, but apparently Dex is about to throw me into the deep end.

"Oh," Dex says, extending a stack of papers to me. "This is the first part of the script. Try to memorize as much of that as you can."

I take the script from him and he smiles at me before dashing out of the trailer.

"Come, sit down."

I sit in the chair and she lowers it to get a better view of exactly what she's doing. I start to flip through the script, quickly reading the highlighted parts as Leslie gets ready. I hear the snip of scissors and I turn my head. Leslie has a devious smile on her face as she comes at me with a comb and some ominous silver scissors.

"I hope you don't mind," she says. "Mr. B is a stickler for real hair in his films."

I take a deep breath. There's no going back now. You can do this. I smile at her and turn back to the script. I hope that she takes her time, because it's going to take me forever to memorize all of these lines.

I catch a glimpse of the first strand of hair falling from my head.

"Have I seen you somewhere before?"

"I just started working for Dex a couple of days ago," I say.

"No... it wasn't here.... Your face just looks so familiar. I'm sure it'll come to me."

I doubt she's ever seen me before... that would be kind of weird given how short of a time I've actually been here.

"Are you from around here?"

"No... I'm from a small town... Greenville... it's kind of near Salem."

"Ah, OK. I've heard of Salem, but not of Greenville. It must be quite the shock for you to be here. I remember when I moved to L.A., it was so exciting."

"Yeah... it's different."

Leslie laughs. I have a feeling that she knows exactly what I'm talking about and there's no need for me to explain myself.

I turn to the third page of the script and read each of the lines three times before turning to the fourth page. Leslie has stopped talking and is humming instead, while she cuts my hair. She must know I need to get cracking on this script.

When she's done cutting my hair, Leslie blows it and styles it... I guess to look like what Dex has in mind for the character. Leslie holds up a mirror to show me.

"What do you think?"

"I love it!"

I was a little nervous, that's for sure, but she did an

amazing job. She cut my hair into an A-line bob that seems to look perfect on me.

"Yay!"

I think Leslie is just as happy as I am. Maybe it has something to do with the fact that I'm easy or at least easy compared to Nicole.

"Now," she says, "let me just put some eye shadow and a few touches of makeup on you. Dex wants your character to have a more natural look."

I nod and set the script on the counter in front of me. Leslie quickly puts the makeup on me, taking maybe five minutes to do what would normally take me at least thirty minutes, and stands back a couple of feet to get a good look at me.

"You look fantastic, Hun."

I smile at her. I'm starting to like Leslie… she seems really nice and seems to have a great attitude.

"Thanks to you."

"Ah! That's where I know you from! You were on TV last night!"

Ugh. It didn't take long for someone to recognize me. I'm just glad that it was a local L.A. station and not something national. I can't imagine everyone in Greenville seeing the segment from last night.

"Yeah…."

"Are you really dating Spencer?"

"No… no."

She grins at me as if she doesn't believe me.

"I'm not," I say.

"Sure, Hun."

"I'm really not, I swear."

"Whatever you say… now get your butt over to wardrobe before you get us both in trouble with Mr. B. It's the next building over."

Leslie starts to hum again as she grabs a broom and sweeps my hair into a neat pile. I give up… I guess she's not going to believe that I'm not dating Spencer. I guess I can't blame her really… the story presented a good case and here I was, on the set of a movie that Spencer is the star of. I don't think I would believe me either if I was her.

I leave the trailer and head toward wardrobe. I hope that I get to see more of Leslie… she's quirky and I like that.

I find the wardrobe building and head inside. There is a woman leaning against the counter with a pen in her hand. As I get closer I can tell she's drawing a dress onto the figure of an outline.

"What do you need?" she says, without looking up from her drawing.

"Dex told me to come here?"

She looks up from her drawing, raises her eyebrow at me and looks me up and down.

"Who are you?"

"Amy."

"Alright, Amy, come with me."

I follow her as she disappears behind a rack of clothes that dwarfs me. It's like the biggest closet in the world. It's crazy. I can't imagine how much all of these clothes cost.

"Try these on."

She hands me a pair of jeans and she goes back to sifting through the rack.

"Is there a dressing room?"

"No. Once we get your size in these clothes, they'll be in your trailer each morning when you arrive on set."

She pulls a white T-shirt off the rack and hands it to me before walking off. I follow her to a wall of shoes. She looks down at my feet and without saying anything pulls a pair of black flats off one of the shelves. She turns to me and stands there staring at me, with the shoes in her hands.

"Well?" she says.

"What?"

"Try the pants on."

"Where should I change?"

"Here."

"Here?"

"Yes, here."

She has a rather no nonsense approach. I give in, figuring this is a one-time thing and the sooner I get it over with the better. I want to suggest that I just tell her my size, but decide against it… I don't want to get on her bad side.

I set the shirt on top of some shoes and quickly pull my own pants down and slip into the jeans she gave me. They are so tight that it's a struggle to get them up and I feel like I can hardly move my legs in them.

"They're really tight. I think I need a bigger size."

"No."

OK….

I pull my shit over my head and toss it on the shelf and put on the T-shirt she gave me. I'm really glad that I wore a white bra today. The shirt is a little looser than the pants, but still tighter than I would have picked out.

"Good," she says, and hands me the flats.

I slip my feet into them and to my surprise the actually fit and they don't feel uncomfortable, like the jeans and the shirt.

"Alright," she says, as she bends down and picks up my shoes and pants from the floor. "I'll have these sent over to your trailer."

"Is that it?"

"Yeah."

She walks a few feet away and disappears down another aisle of clothing racks and she's gone. I manage to find my way through the maze and back to the front door of the building. I head over to the set that I first saw a couple of days ago and Dex is there, getting it ready.

"Hey," he says, when he sees me.

"Hi."

Dex looks me up and down and nods.

"Perfect. I love the outfit… that's exactly what I had in mind for the character."

I smile at him. For the first time since he let Nicole go I can see the genuine joy in his face… it's as if he's finally realizing that I was the right choice and that everything is going to work out. I hope that it does. I want to help him make his dream come true and it feels like for the first time in my life I'm part of something that actually matters to other people and it feels good.

"And I'm loving the hair and minimalist makeup… Leslie nailed it."

Dex tilts his head and looks by me. He smiles and nods and I turn to see who or what he's looking at. It's Spencer and he's walking toward us. Our eyes meet and he smiles at me. I smile back. I can feel my face getting warm and I have to look away from Spencer.

"Hey, Dex. How's it going?"

"Good, good. Amy just finished with wardrobe and makeup and I was just asking her if she was ready to start shooting the first scene."

Spencer nods and turns to me.

"Well… are you ready?"

"I think so," I say.

Spencer puts his hand on my shoulder and I start to feel tingly. I distract myself by looking at the script as I try to memorize the lines.

"Alright," Dex says, turning to the room and raising his voice. "We're ready to shoot the first scene!"

I swallow and look up at Spencer. The look on his face is telling me that everything is going to be alright, but I just don't know… I'm a little worried… I'm a little scared. Here goes nothing.

CHAPTER TWENTY

"Amy?"

I feel a hand on my shoulder, shaking me gently, and I open my eyes. Spencer is standing over me and he smiles as I look into his eyes.

"Hey, sleepyhead."

I yawn and stretch my arms over my head. I can't believe I fell asleep. Well, I guess it's not that surprising after the night of sleep I had last night. Dex stopped shooting for lunch and I decided I wanted to rest a little before we started again and I went to my trailer.

"Are we ready to start again?"

"Nah," Spencer says, as he sits down in the other chair, "it's going to probably be like ten minutes or so. I had a feeling you might be sleeping, so I wanted to come and check on you. I figured it would give you a chance to wake up before we started again."

I nod and look at him… it's not that he's not telling the truth, but I feel like there's another reason for being here, but I'm not going to even ask him.

"Thanks."

I yawn a second time and reach for my bottle of water. I take a long drink and stand up.

"So," Spencer says, "how about that TV show from last night?"

Ugh. I was really hoping that he wouldn't bring that up... ever.... I knew that he would, but I was trying to put it out my mind and here he was, bringing it up right before we had to get back to shooting.

"Yeah... that was something."

"It's funny that they thought we were dating."

What's that supposed to mean? I can't tell by the tone of his voice if he's implying that it's strange because he's out of my league or... I don't even know, it was just a weird and kind of mean thing to say.

"What?" he says.

"I didn't say anything."

"You didn't have to."

"What's that supposed to mean?"

"It's all over your face... you're upset either about what they said on TV or by what I said."

"You can figure it out," I say, glaring at him while taking a sip of water.

Spencer laughs, shakes his head and stands up.

"Look, I wasn't trying to be mean. What I meant was that you've got no interest in me, so it doesn't matter how I feel about you. That's why it was funny that they were implying that we are dating... because I already know I have no shot."

He turns and walks out of my trailer before I can say anything. I sit back down, feeling a little shocked by what he just said. I'm not even sure what to make of it. I didn't think he liked me, not in that way, despite Jess's insistence that he was flirting with me, but it doesn't matter because I have Logan.

There's a knock on my door and my heart starts to race as I wonder if it's Spencer.

"Yeah?"

"Two minutes."

It's not Spencer, and I'm not sure who it is.

"Thanks."

My head is swirling as I try and make sense of what's going on. Was Spencer implying that he does have feelings for me? I never really got that impression. I just assumed that he was being nice to me, especially after I told him the story of how I ended up here.

The only thing I can think of, that really makes sense, is that Spencer is just acting this way as a joke because of the TV show. I don't think it's funny. I really hope he stops because it's already getting old.

This can't go on, it just can't. Not to mention since we are going to be spending a lot of time together working on this movie and I don't want to be irritated with him the whole time.

I grab my script and head out of my trailer, reading the next scene over and over as I walk to the set. I did alright on the first scene, only forgetting my lines a couple of times. We shot the same scene over and over for three hours, so by the time we got done I had my dialogue memorized to the point that I probably will never forget it.

I'm actually kind of surprised that I even got a trailer. I'm not a star like Spencer or Nicole and I'm not as important as Dex. I just kind of figured I would be stuck with some dark dressing room in one of the buildings, but instead I got a nice trailer. Well, it's not as nice as Dex's... but I'm not complaining.

I walk over to Dex, who is talking to Spencer. I flash Spencer a dirty look, which I instantly feel bad about and force myself to smile at him. He smiles back and Dex turns around.

"Alright, you two, are you ready?"

"Yeah," we both say.

"Let's get started then."

Dex seemed quite pleased with how the morning shoot went, which I'm happy about. I hope that I do a good job and that he's pleased with my performance. It's still strange that just a few days ago I was so upset with Dex that I could barely look at him and now I was trying to help him by doing a good job acting. Crazy. It's amazing how quickly things can change.

~~~

"Good work, today," Dex says, pulling the car onto the main road and turning in the direction of the house.

"Thanks."

"You're doing really well for a first timer."

I smile and look over at Dex, but his focus is on driving.

"Good... I hope that you're pleased with casting me."

"I really am. Honestly, when I woke you up this morning I was a little worried still and I don't know why. Maybe it's because of how much this project means to me."

I get it. When I saw him talking to Erin about it I could tell how much it meant to him and I'm still surprised that he's trusted me to be in it. It made me want to do an even better job.

"Good. I hope that I keep doing a good job... I want you to be happy."

He smiles and looks over at me.

"I am... just keep doing what you did today and this movie is going to turn out exactly how I imagined it."

"I'll do my best."

"Thank you, it means a lot to me."

"You're welcome and thank you for trusting me to do this."

He drives in silence for the next few minutes and every time I look over at him he looks deep in thought.

"So," he says, breaking the silence, "I forgot to talk to you about how much I'm going to pay you. I should have said something earlier, but you seemed pleased with how much I was going to pay you to be my assistant, so I didn't think it was a big deal."

"I'm not worried about it… we don't have to talk about it right now if you have other things to think about."

"No, it's fine, I feel like I should tell you what I've been thinking. You know that we were going to pay Nicole forty thousand…."

Dex pauses and takes a left hand turn, his attention drawn back to navigating the L.A. traffic. He can't possibly be planning on paying me that much. I don't care either… even if he paid me half of that I would be over the moon.

"But I'm so happy to be done with her that I was thinking I would pay you sixty thousand and give you one percent of net, too. How does that sound?"

I don't even know what to say. Sixty thousand? I'm in shock.

"Is that alright?" he says.

"Are you sure? That's a lot of money."

He lets out a laugh. I know it's not a lot to him, but I know he's already financing this whole movie himself and he doesn't have to pay me that much.

"I'm very sure and I hope that the movie does well enough that you get something from the net. Do you know what one percent net is?"

"Not really."

I have a guess, but I would rather he explain it to me so that I don't make a fool of myself.

"Basically, if the film does well and we can get it into theaters you will get one percent of all the net profits. So if the movie makes money you make money."

Wow. I don't even know what to say. Is he serious? I can't believe this. It makes me happy that I chose to do this. I know that it's going to cause a setback in terms of going to college, but now if the movie makes money, I'm not going to have to worry about working some stupid job or taking out loans to pay for school.

"Is that alright?" he says.

"That's very generous."

Dex laughs and looks over at me.

"I want to reward you for doing a good job. This way we both can be compensated for our hard work... if people like the movie, that is."

"That makes sense."

"But, just so you know, it can take a long time for an indie film like this to make it to theaters... if it does at all. So don't think about that too much, not right now. That's my advice."

"That makes sense."

"And you're OK with getting paid sixty once we finish?"

"Are you sure it's not too much?"

"Absolutely. I'm going to give Spencer a bump in pay, too, not that he needs it. I just want it to be fair and from what I've seen after one day put me in such a good mood that I think it's justified. The on-screen chemistry between the two of you is just... it's amazing. I've never seen anything like it in all my years in this business."

I don't even know what to say. It's a really nice thing for him to tell me and I'm glad that he feels that way about it... but at the same time I feel a little weird about how people might perceive my relationship with Spencer, on and off screen.

"Thank you. I really appreciate the opportunity."

"You're welcome. I know that it couldn't have been an easy decision, to stay here instead of going back to school, but I'm very glad that you stayed."

He has no idea how hard it was. I still need to talk to Logan about it, although I'm not too worried about it. I have a feeling he will be supportive of it based on the opportunity that Dex has given me.

"Of course... I want to help you make the movie you've been dreaming of."

"Now I just have to tell your mom that you're no longer my assistant, but instead you're starring in my film."

"Yeah… that's going to be *interesting*."

"Don't worry about it, I'll take care of her. You just worry about studying the script for tomorrow's scenes. I made today's shooting schedule unusually light so that didn't feel too overwhelmed, but you handled it like a champ, so tomorrow we are going back to the normal schedule."

I had a feeling he might have done something like that, considering it's only late afternoon, but I'm very glad he did… I feel exhausted. I would have never guessed that acting could be so physically and mentally taxing.

Dex pulls the car through the gate and into the garage. We get out and head for the door that leads into the house, but he pauses with his hand on the handle and turns to me.

"I'm going to go talk to your mom. I think I'll just tell her now and get it over with. I'm assuming you might want to chill out for a little while… so why don't we have dinner at seven?"

"Sounds good."

"I'll let Gina know."

I hadn't thought about it, but I could totally hang out for a little while and decompress from the day. We go inside and Dex goes toward the kitchen and I walk upstairs. I close my bedroom door and flop onto my bed. I take my phone out of my purse and turn it on. I shut it off during the day, not because I was expecting any calls… but I didn't want the temptation of constantly checking to see if Logan had texted me yet.

I wait for it to power on and feel disappointed, again, that there's still nothing from Logan. The only thing that makes it any better is that there's a text from Jess waiting for me.

Hey, what happened to you? I never heard back from you last night.

I totally forgot to text her back once Spencer texted me and I went to the game room to watch the entertainment show. I feel a twinge of guilt… like I should tell her what happened, but I have a feeling that I would never hear the end of it. I really do want to tell her about my role in Dex's movie, but I still want to tell Logan first.

Sorry about that. I totally passed out, it's been a long couple of days. I can't wait to tell you about what's going on, but I still haven't heard back from Logan and I need to tell him first.

I set my phone down on my pillow and force myself to get up. I really want to get out of these clothes. I change into my pajama bottoms and a T-shirt and sit back down. It was nice to change back into my own clothes after wearing jeans and a shirt that were tight, but now I feel really relaxed. Almost relaxed enough that I could just sleep now… but I don't want to miss dinner, not after sleeping through lunch today.

My phone chirps as I get a reply from Jess.

Booo. I want to know what's going on with you, but you're being so secretive.

It's not that… it's just kind of a big thing and I feel like I need to tell Logan about it first so that we can talk about it. I promise I'll tell you as soon as I talk to him

Is everything OK? That sounds kind of ominous and serious.

I reread the text I sent her. She's right, it does kind of sound like that.

Everything is great… in fact it's getting better all the time. I just haven't heard from Logan in a couple of days, so I'm starting to get a little worried, but other than that I'm fantastic.

The more I think about it, the weirder it is that I haven't heard from him… it's just so not like him. Even when he's busy with football he manages to send me a text to check in and see how I'm doing, but there's been nothing for a couple of days now. I try not to let the thoughts enter my mind, but I start to think of all the terrible things that might have happened to him. Maybe he got in a car accident… maybe he got injured again… maybe he met someone else… the list is endless. Thankfully Jess texts me back, which forces me to stop worrying about Logan.

Weird. Well, if I hear anything, I'll let you know. I'm sure it's fine, he's probably just really busy with football.

She's right, I'm sure he's OK. I just needed to hear it from someone else. With everything that's happened in the last couple of months, I tend to assume the worst. I need to stop doing that, especially with how well everything has started to go in the last couple of days.

A knock on my door makes me freeze. I really hope that it's not my mom, coming to yell at me for taking a job that Dex offered me.

"Yeah?" I say.

"Miss Amy? It's me, Gina. There's some mail here for you."

Huh. That's kind of strange. I wonder what it could be… the only thing that comes to mind is the autograph from Logan, but I doubt that it could have gotten here already. I open the door and Gina hands me a large envelope.

"Here you go."

"Thanks."

"Dinner is at seven, just so you know."

"I'll be down."

She nods and smiles at me. I close the door as she walks back toward the stairs. I look at the envelope while walking back to my bed and sit down before opening it.

Inside is a promotional shot of Logan in his pads that he signed for Spencer. Another piece of paper falls out and lands on the floor. I pick up what must be the surprise that Logan told me about… the thing that he sent for me. It's a piece of paper, folded in half. I open it up and read it.

Amy,

You're so special. I can't imagine how my life would have been different if you never walked into the bathroom that day. I know things haven't been easy for you, but I know they are going to get better. I know it in the deepest part of my heart. I'm going to be here to support you in any way that I can, you just have to let me. I can't wait to see your cute face again and kiss your impossibly soft lips.

Love, Logan.

Tears start to form in my eyes as I read the note a second time. He's so sweet. I can't wait to see him either. I feel a little bad that I've delayed our reunion by taking this job, but considering what he wrote in the note about supporting me, I know that he'll understand and be alright with it. I have a feeling he's going to be very happy for me.

I pick up my phone and text Logan.

I just got your note. Thank you so much. It was beautiful. It made me so happy to read it. I can't wait to see you either.

I hit send and just stare at my phone, waiting and hoping that I'll hear back from him. A knock on my door brings me back to reality and I glance at the clock on my wall. It's only six-thirty, so it can't be Gina to tell me dinner is ready. I guess it could be Dex, but it's probably my mom. Whoever it is knocks a second time before I get up and walk over to the door.

I open the door and my mom pushes by me and walks into my room. She turns around and I can see on her face that it's not going to be good. I swallow and close the door.

"How could you?" she says.

I know exactly what she's talking about, but I'm going to play stupid because I don't know exactly what Dex told her.

"What do you mean?"

She puts her hand on her hip and glares at me.

"You auditioned for a role in Dex's movie?"

"Sort of."

"Sort of?"

"Yeah."

"What does that even mean?"

She shakes her head. I can see the rage building in her. I feel bad for Dex… I have a feeling he already caught the brunt of it.

"I didn't audition on purpose."

"What?"

"Spencer, he sort of tricked me into it."

She rolls her eyes and turns toward the window. It's not the first time she's been so mad at me that she won't look at me, and I have a feeling it won't be the last.

"You expect me to believe that? Do you have any idea how stupid that sounds?"

She's right, it does sound kind of crazy, but that's exactly how it happened.

"I swear… you can ask Spencer or Dex."

She sighs and shakes her head.

"You knew how mad I was about you taking the job as his assistant… how did you think I would react when I found out about this?"

"I don't see what the big deal is."

"You don't see what the big deal is? Are you serious? Dex is making this movie with his own money and you auditioned. Of course he cast you… he had no other choice. Now what? You're going to ruin his movie and cost him millions of dollars in the process. Are you ready to shoulder that kind of responsibility?"

"I…."

"I don't give a shit, Amy. Try thinking about someone else for once in your life."

"He said I was good, that's why he cast me."

"Right… I'm sure you're an acting prodigy. I wish your father wouldn't have gotten himself killed. This is all his fault. I wish I never had to bring you here. Now you're going to ruin my life here, too. Great… thanks."

She walks by me and out of my room before I can say anything. I collapse on my bed and push my face into my pillow as the tears start.

Is she right? Did Dex only hire me because he felt obligated to do so? I can't imagine him doing that, but it makes sense now that I think about it. He probably felt guilty about breaking up my parents' marriage and thought maybe he could make me forget about it if he put me in his movie. Is that really the kind of man that Dex is? I just don't know anymore... it seems like everyone always wants something, like it's their only motivation for doing anything. Is that how people really are?

CHAPTER TWENTY-ONE

I look at the clock… fifteen minutes until we are supposed to have dinner. I can't even imagine sitting at a table with my mom and Dex right now… not to mention I've completely lost my appetite.

I walk over to the window and look outside just as the lights for the pool are turning on. It's not dark yet, but the sun is low enough in the sky that it's no longer hitting the pool.

That's what I should do… I should go for a swim. I change into the swimsuit that Spencer bought me, wrap a towel around myself and head downstairs. I poke my head into the kitchen, where Gina is just getting the table set.

"It'll be another five minutes or so, Miss Amy, before everything is ready."

"Oh, actually, I was coming in here to tell you that I'm going for a swim and I'm going to skip dinner…. I'm not feeling that hungry right now."

She opens her mouth, the look on her face says that she wants to protest, but instead she just nods. I smile at her and head outside.

I drop my towel on one of the chairs and walk over to the edge of the pool. I take a deep breath, knowing that the pool is going to be cold, and dive in. The shock of the cold water passes through my body and renders me paralyzed for a moment before I push my feet off the bottom and fill my lungs with air.

I try to just swim, not worrying about anything else, but it doesn't work. All I can think about is my mom and Dex. I wonder what I did to deserve this life? I'm starting to regret being in Dex's movie. I should have known better… my mom is right, I have no acting experience and I should have been able to figure out that he didn't really want me in his film. There's really no other explanation for it. How could I be so stupid?

I only swim five laps before I'm overwhelmed by the need to cry my eyes out. I get out and dry myself off, reaching my room just as the first tears roll down my cheek. I can't do this… I'm starting to feel like I'm going crazy. This can't be what life is really about.

There's a knock on my door and I do my best to ignore it. They knock a second and third time, but I still don't get out of bed. I don't care who it is, I don't want to talk to anyone right now.

My phone chirps a few minutes later and I reach for it in the hope that it's Logan. It's not… it's a text from Dex. I don't care what he has to say, not at this point. I'm starting to feel like maybe I was right about him, the first time when I thought he was just an ass who didn't care about breaking up my family. My phone chirps a second time, it's a second text from Dex and I finally read them.

Amy, I'm sorry about how that all went down. I really want to talk to you so that we can set a few things straight.

I really doubt that he's sorry. If he was sorry, he wouldn't have seduced my mom and broke up my family. Really if it wasn't for Dex everything would have been fine… not to mention Dad would still be alive. I'll never forget that or forgive Dex for what he did. I was momentarily blinded by what I thought was his genuine kindness. I was *so* wrong. I read the next text, not expecting much.

I get that you might be mad at me, but I want the chance to at least explain myself to you. Please, just give me that. If you're still mad at me after… well, then I won't bug you anymore and I'll charter a flight for you back to Salem tonight. You don't have to stay here anymore. I'll deal with your mom, she won't stop you.

I don't know what to say. That's all I wanted all along, so if he's willing to do that for me… maybe I should just talk to him. It would be amazing if I could get back to Salem and Logan. Not to mention it's fairly obvious my mom and Dex would both be happier if I wasn't here. I feel a little bad about Spencer… he's been nice to me for the most part, but I can't force myself to be miserable just for his sake.

Fine, I'll talk to you.

I set my phone down as I wait for a reply. I get up and get my clothes that I brought with me and the bags that I packed them in. I want to be ready to leave as soon as I'm done talking to Dex. I don't want to be here any longer than I have to be.

As I start to pack there's a knock on my door. I take a deep breath and try to mentally prepare myself for a talk with Dex. I open the door and Dex is standing there, with a solemn look on his face and car keys in his hand. He looks me up and down and I suddenly realize that I'm standing in front of him wearing just my swimsuit. I quickly close the door and change into the clothes that I wore earlier. Normally I would be freaked out, and embarrassed by that, but at this point I know that I'm leaving tonight and I don't care.

I open the door and walk into the hall. I don't see Dex, so I head downstairs. He's standing by the door to the garage and turns and goes into it when he sees me. I follow him and get into the passenger seat as he starts the car.

"What are we doing?" I say.

"I want to talk to you, but I don't want your mom around."

He pulls the car out of the garage, through the gate and takes a left.

"So, what did you want to talk about?"

I want to get this done with as soon as possible. I just hope that he keeps to his word about getting me a flight out of here tonight.

"Don't act so eager. I want you to hear what I have to say… and after that if you still want to leave I'll call and have a flight waiting for you. I'll drive you home and by the time we can get your things together the plane will be waiting."

He looks over at me and I nod.

"There's some things that I'm not totally clear on, so I want to figure them out first," he says.

"Alright."

Dex takes a left turn onto one of the main roads in Beverly Hills and takes a deep breath. I look over and I can see the tormented look on his face. I wonder why it looks like this is eating away at him… it really shouldn't be… he's to blame for all of this as far as I'm concerned.

"So… I want to tell you how the events in Greenville went down, according to me. I met your mother, she was standing in the front of one of the crowds for a whole week of shooting before I ever worked up the courage to go talk to her. She was really nice and I thought she was beautiful. I asked her out to dinner and we spent a few afternoons and nights together during the last couple of weeks of shooting. I realized, as we were getting ready to head back here, that I had fallen in love with her and I asked her to come with me. She agreed and never mentioned to me that she was married or that she had a daughter. She never told me she didn't, but I sort of assumed that she would have said something… but she didn't. When your dad died… that was… that was the first time I'd heard about him, or you for that matter. I insisted that you should come here even before she felt like she didn't want the liability of you doing whatever she thought you would be doing."

Dex pauses as he takes another turn and merges into traffic. I can't believe what he's saying. I don't know whether or not to believe him... it's hard for me to think he has any reason to lie, but why would my mom do that? Is she really capable of doing that? I look over at Dex and I can see in his face that he's telling the truth.

"I just found out the truth about all of that earlier tonight... she spilled it when she got mad at me for casting you in the movie."

It's so amazing... how could she do that? It's so messed up. I want to go back to the house and scream at her. All this time, every minute that I've been here, I've been mad at Dex for breaking up my family, when really she's the one to blame.

"I'm sorry," I say.

"For what?"

"I... I've been rude and inappropriate to you since the moment I got here. I've been blaming you for destroying my family, this whole time, and I feel just awful about it. I had no idea that she had been so *deceptive* and that she's really the one to blame."

Dex lets out a deep sigh, pulls the car into an empty spot on the side of the road turns the car off. He looks over at me and takes my hand in his and looks into my eyes.

"I'm very sorry, Amy, I really am. If I had known... I... I would never asked her to come with me. I could never knowingly cause that much trauma to a family."

He lets go of my hand and wipes a tear from his own cheek. I start to cry, too. He takes a deep breath as he tries to calm himself.

"And... I want you to know that I hired you as my assistant because I thought you would do a good job. When Spencer asked me to let you audition, I tried to talk him out of it because I didn't want to put that kind of pressure on you and I knew already that your mom would freak out because she was already mad about you being my assistant."

I thought that it was a little crazy that my mom flipped out when she found out about that....

"And... I'm glad that I listened to Spencer and gave you an audition because you are perfect for the role. You're a thousand times better than Nicole. I'm glad that I let her walk... it's the best thing that's ever happened to me. When I first set out to make this film... I wanted you to be in it, I just hadn't met you yet. So, no matter what your mom said, you're perfect for the role and I'm so excited to have you in it."

I knew in my heart that when he told me he wanted me in his film it was the truth. When my mom suggested otherwise I know why it upset me... not because I believed her, but because I knew deep down that she was wrong and Dex cast me because he wanted me in his movie.

The hatred that I had felt toward Dex, from when I thought he ruined my family, is now directed at my mom. How could she do this? Is this the kind of person that she is? I don't want to ever see her again. She doesn't deserve to have a guy like Dex in her life.

"What happens now?" I say.

"That's up to you. I've said everything that I wanted to tell you... now you just need to decide what you want. If you want to go to Salem, I can't blame you... I'd want to get as far away from *her* as possible if I were you. I still want you in my film though and the only solace I can offer is that if you stay we can make a truly beautiful piece of cinema together. I know we can."

I want to run away... run back to Salem and have Logan hold me, but I don't know. I want to be a part of Dex's movie... he's given me such a wonderful opportunity that I feel like I have to take it. It would be a shame to waste that.

I turn to Dex and look into his eyes. I can see the

respect he has for me on his face and I can tell that he's not pleading with me to stay… but allowing me to make the decision on my own. I have a feeling that even though he's adamant about me being in his movie, he would support whatever I decide to do.

It makes me sad to think that this side of Dex was there since the moment I first met him and I chose to ignore it. I guess there's no time like the present to embrace what we have.

"I'll do it. Let's make movie history. I want people to watch our film and feel how you feel about it. I want to share in your passion."

A smile crosses his face and he nods. Dex starts the car and makes a U-turn at the next intersection.

"I promise you won't regret it."

Usually, I would be skeptical of that kind of promise, but I can hear in his voice that he truly believes what he's saying and he's going to do everything in his power to not let me down… and not let himself down.

"What about my mom?"

Dex is silent for the rest of the drive and only speaks as we wait for the gate at the house to open.

"Let me worry about her. She's going to have to come to terms with the fact that I want you in my film."

Dex pulls into the garage and turns off the car.

"Thank you," I say.

"No, thank you for listening to me and helping me with this film. I haven't been this excited to work since my first day on set."

He flashes me a smile and winks as we walk inside.

"I'm going to go upstairs and see if I can get some sleep," I say.

"Good. It's been a long day, I'm sure you need the rest. I'll see you in the morning."

I walk upstairs and Dex heads into the kitchen. I close my door and sit down on my bed. I have to tell Jess what's been going on… I can't wait anymore. I grab my phone to text her, but there's a text from Logan waiting for me. I feel a wave of relief pass over my body now that I know he's OK. I was starting to really worry about him.

Stop texting me. I was hoping that we could wait to have this conversation until you were back in Salem… but I can't take it any longer. We have to take some time off while you figure out what you want. I thought that you were content with being with me, but we both know that's not the case.

Tears start to roll down my eyes. Is he breaking up with me in a text? Why would Logan do this to me? And what does he mean by *we both know that's not the case*? I want to throw my phone across the room and pretend that I never read the text from him. I quickly type a reply and hit send.

I don't know what you're talking about. I'm so happy to be a part of your life and I thought that you felt the same way. I know we didn't have much time together, but I thought we had a special connection.

My phone vibrates before I can even start to think about what to do.

I thought so too. And the fact that you had the audacity to ask for my autograph for him… that was just the cherry on top of it all. I can't believe you. I thought you were different from all the other girls, but now… now I know that you're the same as the rest of them… as soon as you find a better guy you can't move on quickly enough. I saw the story, it's all over YouTube, so don't pretend like you don't know what I'm talking about.

Oh god. Logan saw the video where they showed me out with Spencer and implied that we were dating. I hadn't even thought about him seeing it.

Please, you have to believe me… it's not what it looks like. There's nothing going on between me and Spencer. I swear. Please.

I know what I saw.

Logan, I swear. I don't have any feelings for him.

If that's true, then we can talk about it when you come back to school in a couple of weeks. Until then I think it would be best if we didn't talk or text so that neither of us says something we might regret.

I don't know what to tell him. If I tell Logan that I'm not going back to Salem, at least not until we finish filming, he's never going to believe me. I set my phone down and drop my head into my hands as my whole body shakes with each sob. I have to tell Logan, he deserves to know. I grab my phone and text him back.

I got cast in a movie, so I'm not sure when I'm coming back… but I know that it won't be before the start of the school year.

Really Amy? You expect me to believe that nothing's going on between you and that guy, but you're not coming back? You're a piece of work. Seriously. Have a nice life.

I throw my phone to the floor and it bounces and hits the wall. I'm pretty sure I broke it and I don't care. There's nothing else I could say to Logan, not in a text or a phone call.

I feel so alone. I wish I could just go to sleep and never wake up again.

~~~

Thank you for reading Tainted Love. I hope you enjoyed it and that you'll want to read the next book. If you want to be notified when the next book is out, or when I release anything new, join my mailing list. Simply visit http://eepurl.com/xbe7z

Also, if you want to find out more about me or my other books, please visit my website http://www.emmakeene.com

ABOUT THE AUTHOR

I live in beautiful Seattle, WA with my amazing, supportive husband and our two German Shepherds that truly believe it's all about them. I love the rain and it gives me plenty of time to read and write.

Made in the USA
Charleston, SC
13 April 2016